The Portable Son

[stories]

By Barrett Hathcock

Published by Aqueous Books
P.O. Box 12784
Pensacola, FL 32591
www.aqueousbooks.com
All rights reserved.
Published in the United States of America
ISBN: 978-0-9826734-8-5
First edition, Aqueous Books printing, November 2011
Book design and layout: Cynthia Reeser

Aqueous Books

Acknowledgments for
The Portable Son:

For their help and friendship during the long writing of this book, I thank Wes Meador, Michael Martone, Wendy Rawlings, Harry Thomas, Aaron Welborn, Marshall Boswell, Scott Esposito, and John Miller.

I am particularly indebted to Cynthia Reeser, who built a home for this book.

Versions of some of these stories were previously published elsewhere: "High Cotton" in *Fried Chicken and Coffee*; "Timber Walking" in the *Arkansas Review*; "Nightswimming" in *[sic] magazine*; "Popular Baggage" in *Louisiana Literature*; "Baggage Claim" (as "Crush") in the *Cimarron Review*; and "The Portable Son" in *REAL: Regarding Arts & Letters*. I am grateful to these journals and their editors.

Dedication

To my mother and father, for bearing me.
To Katie, for bearing with me.

Contents

We never knew we could want more than that out of life.

—*Billy Joel*

High Cotton

When they cotton dive, the boys become serious. They coil into themselves, squatting on the lip of the metal cotton bins, and they thrust their bodies into the air. The boys go for distance, they go for height, but their main concern is arc. They're trying to pierce the cotton deeply and completely. Against the sunset, they curve together like dolphins into the ocean, and the cotton catches and folds around them as they disappear beneath, swimming into the soft waves, bits of husk floating by their bodies like shells. They do this over and over, pulling themselves back up to the lip of the bins and hurling themselves off again. The bins grunt under the pressure. The boys dive until their arms and legs ache. In midair, wisps of cotton flutter from their hair and float behind them like bits of sea foam.

When they were 16, this was their routine.

❦

Though the boys were physically distinguishable—Jeremy, tall and dusky; Peter, dirty-blond—together they acted like a mechanically simple but efficient machine, first the tall body, then the short, moving together through their high school lives, chewing through each new day, benefiting from the symbiotic advantage of two heads, four feet, four hands, four eyes. They had been friends since the fourth grade, though they never considered how or when the friendship started. It simply existed. They might well have been fraternal twins for the way they finished each other's sentences, inhabited and discarded each other's clothes, were fed and parented in each other's houses.

❦

The diving always made them late. For Peter, dinner was at six, precisely. His grandfather, bitter and enfeebled, had always had his dinner straight up at six, and he wasn't going to change just because he was forced to live with his goddamned daughter, Peter's mother. As part of the family agreement, the old man had given up his car—a mid-'80s Lincoln Town Car, a midnight blue monster that Peter did his best to rag out. Jeremy, whose mother was still litigating the proper amount of alimony out of his own father, was without a car and rode with Peter everywhere.

Peter always knew they had to get home, but he was loath to leave the cotton bins, which they had found one afternoon while riding around the farmland north of Niskayuna High. The bins were huddled together in the corner of a cotton field, metal boxes of bleached orange peeling to rust. After diving, Peter liked to smoke while reclining, delicately flicking his ashes out through the finger-thick holes of the wire mesh, intent on not staining the cotton with his ash. Jeremy, on the other hand, was an incorrigible napper and liked to be submerged, the cotton tucked up to his chin. At an impossibly long distance away, his bare toes protruded.

At school, cotton had become a code word. Whenever they saw girls walking by, girls they knew or wanted to know, girls in boots and belts, sweaters and pullovers, fleeces with and without hoods, the girls became "like cotton."

"Just like cotton," Jeremy would say with a contained smile.

"Fresh warm cotton at two o'clock," Peter would say.

"Very uncotton," Peter would sometimes say.

After a dive, no matter how late, Peter would drive home slow and take the back roads into Jackson and roll down the windows and sometimes Jeremy would dial the soul station run out of Gluckstadt and they would listen to Al Green and smell the farmers grilling out behind their houses.

ନ

If, looking back, Peter had had to trace the beginning of Jeremy and Lina's relationship, he would have said it began at a party at Robert Birch's house in the winter of their sophomore year, not too long after that first cotton-diving season had ended. She was sitting on a couch in the living room, her legs folded under her Indian-style. A half-finished can of Beast rested between her legs. Peter noticed how the sweat of the can left damp marks on the inside thigh of her jeans. They had a button fly, shiny like new nickels. Lina was short with long black hair that mysteriously contained surprising strands of brown, and sometimes red, depending on the light. She was dark, even in the winter, and when the couples walked among each other at basketball games in February, it was obvious she wasn't from around there. All the Mississippi girls had lost their brown, gone back to pearly white skin, tan lines gone for a few more months. Lina was from down further south, though the boys did not know where. She was telling some story, surrounded by other girls, gesturing with her one free hand and using the other to hold the beer steady between her legs.

"So like ro I am so not kidding that boy was fucking wasted," Lina said.

She was famous around the school, although no one discussed why. All the boys who had been there at Niskayuna since seventh grade knew who she was, and remembered the day they first noticed her, the day she was pulled out of the junior high tableaux. Lina was the girl who had her first period publicly, during morning break, as she ate an apple on one of the picnic tables out in front of the quad. Nobody remembers the actual scene as it happened. They only remember the small spot of blood that stained the picnic table bench. Lina went home early. Nobody ever questioned her about the incident or gave her a hard time. Nobody said anything. Though the junior high boys would never confess to this, most of them stopped by the table at some point during the day. They approached slowly, with the rolling crunch of gravel under their feet, and they stretched their necks out and looked down at the spot of blood, making sure not to bend over, not to get too close. They stood there looking at it for a minute and let out a breath, recognizing that what they had heard was true. They then turned around and crunched back to their class, or their friends, or their mothers waiting for them in their cars.

"What the hell does 'ro' mean?" asked Peter, later that night back in the car.

"I think it might be short for 'bro,'" said Jeremy.

"That's stupid. Is that some sort of Florida thing?"

"Lighten up, Pete." Jeremy lit another cigarette and spent the rest of the evening looking out the window, finally asking around midnight to be taken home, even though his mom was out of town, and he could have done anything, and could have done it all night.

ᘏ

Peter's full name was Peter Allen Traxler. He called the car the Traxler Town Tank, "a couch on wheels handed down through generations." When he drove people home from parties—he was always looking for an excuse to drive—he'd throw his arm up on the seat and crane his head backward and say, "Welcome to the finest automotive contraption in Northeast Jackson. Don't worry about your safety"—and at this point he'd let go of the wheel and completely turn to the backseat passengers, Jeremy manning the steering—"if we hit anything, we'll probably come out all right."

ᘏ

On some weekend nights, months into their relationship, depending on the schedule of the evening, Jeremy and Lina would make out in the Tank. If there was a party, Jeremy would snatch away Peter's keys as he stood pumping up the keg, or if they went to a movie, Lina and Jeremy would take a long trip for snacks. Since both houses were on "permanent lockdown," Jeremy claimed, they made time where they could. Once, when Lina's father had to make an emergency business trip in the middle of a week, Jeremy begged Peter into driving him over to Lina's house. Peter did his homework out in the car, hunkered beside the window to get the good streetlight, precal notes spread across the dash.

☙

In their second year of diving, junior year, their technique became more intricate, involving flips and twists and convoluted and ultimately foiled landings. Daylight Savings Time was about to end, and the specter of a 5:20 sunset haunted Peter. He whined about it at school so much Jeremy had to tell him to shut up before someone got curious.

The boys also became self-aware of their diving. They became finicky and pedantic about the details of the dive. They were harsh in their critiques of each other's performance. They developed rules: you must always cotton dive shirtless. You must wait at least 48 hours after a rain. Sunset is the optimal time to dive, but full-on darkness is too dangerous. You should never cotton dive alone. Each person should act as the other's lifeguard. You must check in with your diving partner after every dive to ensure he has not smothered.

Then, one day, while standing on the edge of a bin, psyching up for a backflip, Peter took off his shorts.

After landing, he began victoriously swishing his arms and legs in that way people do when they're making angels in the snow.

"What in the hell are you doing?" asked Jeremy, who had turned around to Peter's bin.

"I don't know," said Peter.

"You don't have any clothes on."

"Yeah, but—"

"Put your fucking shorts on."

"Yeah, but Jeremy, it feels—"

"I don't fucking care. *Put* your shorts on."

"Why?"

"Because it's against the rules, that's why."

Peter glared at him for a moment, then reached for his shorts and grunted out a *fine*.

"Oh, shit—Goddamn it. Put your pants on."

"That's what I'm doing. Jesus," said Peter.

No!" screamed Jeremy, his voice cracking. He was diving for his shirt and shoes.

On the horizon, a tornado of dust funneled behind a pickup truck. It was speeding along the road next to the strip of thorny trees that led to the bins. "Maybe he isn't coming—" began Peter. The furious cloud of dust only grew. The truck was coming right for them. The boys busted it. Peter had never dressed so fast. The boxers and shorts went on as one. Belts and buttons and zippers were left undone. Feet were stuffed into untied shoes. Shirts were on inside-out. Socks were crammed into pockets. And everything was accompanied by Jeremy's wail:

"Get in the car hurry up I can't believe we're gonna get busted for this shit I hope he didn't see your naked ass we are so dead oh my God would you just hurry the fuck *up*." The Tank tore away. The pickup was about fifty yards behind them. You could have seen the dust for miles. They drove so fast that the speedometer—a bright orange toothpick—peaked out at 80 and stuck there vibrating. The car shook and the wind gushed through the open windows and pummeled them. Three minutes later when they swerved through the gate at the school and parked behind the observatory, Jeremy pronounced the coast clear.

ᚱ

Peter heard his mother come into his bedroom early to put away clean clothes, the socks and boxer shorts and generic white undershirts. She did not do this quietly, the warped dresser drawers needing two hands, their metal pulls clinking when slammed shut. Peter pretended to sleep. She let out a heavy sigh, a sigh that Peter recognized as his mother's trademark, a theatrical expression of her martyrdom. He wasn't sure—lying there encased in the down comforter—if she was sighing because of him, or his father, or his Grandpa. Same difference, he thought.

"What's this?" she said. "What's this?"

Peter feigned sleep. She had picked up Peter's dirty clothes that had been shed in a wad next to his bed, peeling undershirts out of knit shirts, boxers out of khaki pants. Peter mentally inventoried all the contraband he could remember. Cigarettes and lighter? Wedged underneath his car seat. Plastic traveler-sized bottle of Southern Comfort? Wrapped in a Piggly Wiggly bag and bundled with the spare-tire gear in his trunk. The half-smoked dimebag of pot bought from Binc Wilson? Was in the car, now given to Jeremy to hide at his house once he heard rumor of drug dogs patrolling the Upper School lot. String of six condoms acquired two years ago at camp? In the Lincoln's glove compartment, hidden inside the owner's manual. Three consecutive issues of early '93 *Penthouse*? Accidentally thrown out the fall before, still sad about it. Peter could think of nothing else.

"Peter, what's this?" his mother said, her sad presence now sitting on his bed, impossible to ignore.

"Mom?" he said, emerging, playing his best. "That you? What's up?"

"Peter, what's this? It fell out of your clothes."

She held a tuft of raw cotton in her hand. Peter, dramatically groggy, worked at the wicks of his eyes with his fingers until they squeaked, and leaned over her hand, breathing hard. He tried somehow to reverse the blushing; he could feel the heat rush up his throat and over his cheeks. His lips felt chapped. He tasted the rusty morning taste in his mouth. Fabulous excuses began developing in his mind, intricate plots involving car wrecks and hospitals and emergencies and trauma.

"I dunno. Is it lint or something?" he said.

"It's not lint, honey. This is cotton. Like the kind you pick off a bush."

Peter just kept staring at her hand, its fine wrinkles like the depthless cracks seen on old paintings.

"I dunno, Mom. Where did you get it?"

"It was in your clothes—where did you and Jeremy go last night?"

"Just the game. Like we always do."

The hand retracted. The lint clutched tight, her face a blank hardness.

"Did we win?"

"No. Of course not," Peter said, coughing up a laugh. "They beat us like a drum."

"Wonderful," his mother said. She got up, leaving the rest of the clean clothes stacked next to Peter in a neatly squared pile, the lock of cotton caught tight in her hand.

That next week, without explanation, Peter inherited his father's cell phone. "Just in case something comes up," his mother said.

ᏟᏚ

"I had a strange afternoon," Jeremy said.

He looked off to the horizon, the way Peter had seen people in movies do when they are about to expel a great secret. They were on their way to a Halloween party.

"It was different. Like nothing else. Ever."

Jeremy was very solemn when he spoke. He was dressed as Ricky Martin, with squeaky leather pants that Peter insisted were too shiny and radiant to be merely leather, that the pants were either pleather or vinyl. Vinyl, pleather, whatever, Jeremy had said. It ain't cotton. He wore a tight, cream-colored shirt. Neither tried to identify its material. It was collarless but had a diagonal slit at the throat-line that flapped open at will in a way that Peter said was either distinctly Ricky Martin or distinctly Vulcan.

"*What* is so different?" asked Peter.

"Can you keep a secret?" asked Jeremy. Peter nodded automatically. "I was there when you came by this afternoon."

"So why didn't you come to the door?"

"Well, Lina was there, too. But no one else was around. So, you know, we started to make out."

"Yeah?"

"And well, we went ... further."

"You did it? Oh." Peter was at a total loss. He was dressed in his normal clothes. He didn't have a costume but an injury; a fake, rubber screw was glued onto his forehead with trickles of blood dried down his face and throat. His grandfather had said it was so lifelike that he wanted to vomit. Peter was proud and asked for pictures.

"No no no. We didn't do it. I told you that we are not going to do it for a while. Not until we've been going out for at least a year. We just said we loved each other like a month ago."

"But—"

"We didn't. We just. Well ..."

"Well, what?"

"I don't want to say it."

"Why not?"

"Well, it sounds so cheap when you just blurt it out."

"Aw, J, come *on*." They were quiet. Peter checked his screw. It still looked perfect—blood spreading like branches across his face. It had tickled horribly when his mother squeezed the fake blood out of the dropper. But it had tasted oddly sweet, as if sugared. He glanced over at Jeremy, whose hair was a caramel bouffant. Peter wondered if he would try to carry the impersonation completely through the party that night. He had been practicing.

"What's she going as?" Peter asked.

"Huh?" And then after a moment, he said, "Oh, yeah. She's going to be a geisha girl."

"A geesha girl? What's that?" asked Peter.

"I don't really know. Some oriental thing."

"So are you going to tell me?" Peter asked, sounding more eager than he had intended. They were almost at the house. He could see the cars half-parked on the lawn.

"Listen, just ..." Jeremy crossed his arms. Peter pulled up and killed the engine. The house thumped with faint music.

Jeremy stuck his right hand into Peter's face. "Sniff," he said. Peter knitted his brows. "Do it. Sniff."

Peter inhaled. Jeremy's index and middle fingers floated under his nose for a brief moment.

They were both quiet. And then Peter said: "That's way better than cotton."

CO3

The party was lame. The boys mulled around on the back porch. Their breath was the same white cloud as their cigarette smoke. Lina and Marianne, Peter's date, were somewhere inside. Around eleven it started to sleet.

"Do you think she wants to?" Peter asked. They were standing under the overhang of the roof. Peter's sneakers were slowly soaking. The hem of his jeans was damp, as if he had been running through tall, wet grass.

"I don't know. Probably. Maybe," Jeremy said.

"How can you tell?"

"I don't know. Maybe she'll say something."

"You could say something."

"Oh, yeah." And when he noticed that Peter wasn't kidding, he said, "But how?"

"What do you mean 'how'? You must have talked about this some."

"No, I mean where? As you well know, I have no car."

"Your house?" Peter said.

"With my parents? Are you kidding? My mom hears it when the dog farts. She's up checking to see if it's a burglar. We can't get halfway through a movie, for chrissakes."

"Hers?"

"No. Her father dates."

"I think I've seen him. Homecoming?"

"Yeah. He was her escort."

"How did someone so tall have someone that short?"

"Lay off."

"Okay, I'm sorry. I'm just saying that if you ever had kids, they might be tiny."

"Pete."

"Okay, sorry."

"Let's not even go there."

"Well, have you thought about that?"

"Yes. *Duh.*"

"So?"

"So ... I got some condoms."

"Good. What kind?"

"I can't remember."

"What do you mean you can't remember? It's not that hard. They're either—"

"I haven't actually gotten them yet."

"Well, you need to."

"I know," said Jeremy. "I am. I will."

Peter caught himself glaring at Jeremy, as if he was squeezing the agreement out of him. His bouffant had lost its shape and it was just regular Jeremy hair now, except lit with the glittery hair-paint Lina had bought him. The sleet was coming down heavier. It sounded like bits of plastic falling. The blood on his face had begun to itch.

"Is she on the pill?" asked Peter.

"Has been since she was fourteen."

"Fourteen? What for?"

"I don't know. It like helps them with their thing. You know."

"It does? How?"

"I don't know—I heard it somewhere."

Peter, after smirking disbelief for a moment, said, "Has she been screwing around since she was fourteen?"

"Peter. Goddamn it. Why do you say shit like that?"

There was a knock on the sliding glass door behind them. It was Lina, her face ghostly white in the make-up. Her hair had come down, too. It had been up, intricately braided and folded, and Peter had told her she looked like origami. Her small smudge of lipstick and the white paint around her mouth had faded from the drinking, so she looked like she was in reverse black face. *Let's go*, she mouthed to Jeremy.

"Now?" he asked. She nodded and mouthed, *please?* He said okay and held up his cigarette, only burned a fourth of the way down. She mouthed *okay* and her floating ghost-face disappeared back into the house.

"She's been on the pill since—" said Peter.

"Shut up," Jeremy whispered. "It's a fucking miracle I don't kick your ass."

Peter started stamping his feet. His legs felt numb from the calves down. "You couldn't even try, Ricky."

"How would you like it if I said something like that?"

"All I'm saying," Peter said, still stomping, "is that you should ask how many partners she's had."

"Why?"

"Because it's important."

Peter was now bent over rubbing his shins. The rhythmic sound of his hands on his jeans. He couldn't help but think of what this weather was doing to the cotton. It was probably turning into oatmeal and would take days to dry enough for another jump. And before they knew it, it would be Thanksgiving.

"What in the hell are you doing, Peter?"

"My feet are practically frozen solid," he said.

"Well why didn't you say something?" asked Jeremy.

"Because you said you wanted to stay out here."

"But not if you are freezing to death."

"Are you pissed at me?"

"*No,*" said Jeremy. "It's just this night has so completely *sucked.*"

"Well, maybe we could—"

There was another knock on glass, much harder. They both turned around. *Now,* she mouthed.

"Okay," Jeremy said back. Peter heard him curse under his breath and saw him drop his cigarette into his beer can and swish it around like Peter'd seen cousins do. It was nearly finished anyway. But Jeremy didn't move, only stood there looking at the glass door. He was probably watching Lina walk, Peter thought. She had been wearing a kimono but ended up borrowing someone's sweat pants after about 20 minutes. At school, she had a way of positioning herself at the front of whatever group of girls she was walking with so that you could always see her, despite her shortness.

Peter remembered how she squatted down, like a catcher, to get her books for each class. She didn't carry her backpack compulsively like the other students. She carried only the books she needed for the next class, propping them on her hip. (Because of some unspoken tradition, the lockers at Niskayuna

High were mostly decorative.) When she squatted down, her shirt would sometimes separate from the waistline of her pants, so that there was a band of flesh uncovered, the amount depending on the type of shirt and pants. Peter had seen her shrink down to replace a binder, a highlighter, a copy of *Othello*, and when the portion of her lower back had appeared, he had once seen, just above the waistline, a glitter of metal. At first he didn't know what it was and he tried to stare inconspicuously while fiddling with his locker. But as she moved, the belly-chain moved, and the light reflected off it again as if the metal were jeweled. Peter stepped closer to peer down at what he thought looked like a necklace. He was almost over her, trying to decipher exactly what was tied around her waist, exactly what it was composed of. Then she stood up. Peter straightened and stepped back, suddenly self-aware. Lina walked off to her class without turning around. All Peter could now see were jeans and a sweater.

"Jeremy," Peter said. "Come on. Let's go." He stood behind Jeremy, waiting for him to slide open the door. Jeremy was still looking into the glass, into his reflection. Peter gave him a little push, very soft, just under his right shoulder blade. After a second push, Peter felt him un-tense, and he finally slid the door open and the boys walked into the warm, dry party together.

ോ

After Daylight Savings passed, their trips to the cotton bins became short and intense. They had seen the pickup once more, pulling up a dust storm on the horizon as they'd pulled off the road. It had turned toward them, so Peter gunned it back onto the road. But they still returned, only once or twice a week, one of them standing on the edge of a bin, fully clothed, the car keys held tight, keeping watch, while the other jumped and whooped and flipped and cursed the farmer, wherever he was. Peter typically took the first lookout.

◌

Now that it was getting dark early, Peter's mom wanted him home first thing after school. He needed to bring his grades up, she'd said. He had come home the week before with a scratch on his nose he couldn't explain. He had scratched himself on a cotton bulb husk, but he was sure she thought it was Drugs.

Jeremy was out sick and Peter had been driving around Niskayuna after school, thinking about going diving solo but always deciding it was too risky. He would get home by four and his mother would ask where he'd been, and he couldn't even come up with a good lie. She knew Jeremy was sick and trusted Peter even less alone.

After three days of his mumbled evasions, she said, "What part of come home right after school don't you understand? Either get home or give me the keys."

The next day after school, walking out to his car, Peter saw Lina waiting at the curb amidst the backpacks and the baseball hats.

"Need a ride?" asked Peter. She shook her head. She was in a black skirt that touched the tops of her knees. A black sweater buttoned twice over a sky blue stretchy shirt. Her hair blew in the wind and a strand stuck to her lip.

"My dad's coming. He's bringing me my car." And then as an explanation she said, "It's my birthday tomorrow."

"*Oh*. Happy birthday. Jeremy hadn't told me. You're getting a car?"

"Mhmm. A 4Runner."

"Sweet," said Peter. "You talk to Jeremy?"

"Still sick."

"Bummer. I haven't seen him in like a week."

"How do you go on?"

"What?"

"Nothing."

"Why do you hate me so much?" he asked.

"I don't hate you at all."

"Right."

The flow of cars kept running through the carpool line with a stuttery consistency, like the time-lapsed photography of blood circulation he'd seen in biology earlier that day.

"What's he getting you?" Peter said.

"I don't know," she said. "I hope he just gets well enough to go out. His mom keeps saying he's got mono."

"Really?"

"Ro, I totally did not give him mono. Don't even joke."

"I didn't say that. I wasn't even gonna."

A hunter-green 4Runner was making its way around the curve of the entrance road. Lina's hair swirled around her face in the wind. It looked almond-colored in the bright November sun, Peter thought.

"So that it?" Peter asked.

She nodded, her excitement undisguised.

"That's really nice," Peter said.

"Thanks. Maybe when J gets better, we can all go out. I'll drive."

"That would be nice. Is it a four-wheel drive?"

"I have no idea. You could ask my dad."

"Nah. Just curious. If it was we could take it mudding."

"I don't think so," she said.

The truck pulled up in front of them and Lina put her stuff in the backseat and then did a sort of hop to get into the front passenger's seat. She made some indecipherable, excited noise to her father. She gave a quick wave before closing the door, and Peter waved back, but by then the door was closed, the glass tinted, the truck pulling away, and Peter was left alone in the carpool line, another car pulling up and jolting to a stop and another person jumping in and leaving.

Ↄ

The next day, a Friday afternoon, was perfect for cotton diving. The air was crisp; the sky was cloudless, a deep, blinding blue. Peter sat out on his back porch smoking a cigarette. His mother was happy. He'd finally come home straight from school. She gave him an exaggerated *thank you* before leaving for the store, said she'd make him one of his favorites—chicken and dumplings—for finally listening.

Jeremy was still out of school. Peter had tried to find Lina, to see what the game plan was for the weekend, but no luck. It was getting close to five, and he was growing desperate from the lack of communication and the vision of Friday night at home with the family, watching Grandpa's mouth work on the dumplings at dinner, Dad turning up *Nash Bridges* too loud. He started another cigarette and called Jeremy.

Jeremy's mother was startled to hear from him. "Yes, Peter. He's doing much better. Doctor gave him a shot yesterday.

Turned out not to be mono—just a bad cold, I guess. Anyway, he told me he was with you," she said.

Peter tried to cover, but his voice went shaky, and he could tell from the way hers became thin and angular that she did not believe anything he said.

He called Lina's house. He felt odd doing this. He had seen Jeremy do it so many times. The number-pattern was not familiar but the sound of their touch-tone keys was comforting. The voice of a very large man answered. She was out, for her birthday. She would not be in until late. Peter beeped off the portable phone and began to pace. It was almost five. Three cigarette butts lay crushed in black, ashy smudges at his feet on the back porch. His mother would be home soon with the dumpling mix. Birds chirped. Everything outside turned a shade darker, as if the world had just slightly condensed. The old man was out with her, riding shotgun, guarding all the coupons, reading the obituaries, telling her to slow down. Leaves were turning orange, a purplish-brown. It was four forty-five. Thanksgiving was two weeks away. He dialed Jeremy's cell phone. It rang and rang, went to voicemail. He imagined it bleating next to him, sitting on the seat against his thigh, wherever he was. He re-dialed.

Ȣ

They measured the circumference of the four bins with their feet, one placed carefully in front of the other. Jeremy took off his shirt, his watch, his shoes, his socks, his belt, his jeans, his boxers, one leg at a time so as not to fall. Lina began undressing as well, sandals flipped over the side, T-shirt on the edge of the bin, bra thrown back toward the truck, jeans unbuttoned—the delicate tambourine jingle of the button fly—sliding off the left leg, then the right, holding her hand out to Jeremy for balance. She tossed the jeans over the edge. She wore no underwear. A thin wire sparkled around her waist. She pranced away from Jeremy on the balls of her feet. The bin whined underneath, and Jeremy followed her out to the center, to the cross created by the conjoined bins. They embraced, their two vague shadows momentarily congealing. Holding hands, standing side-by-side, they turned to face one of the bins. After glancing at each other, they leaned back, together, falling backwards into the cotton, swimming in back strokes. Again, over and over, together or on their own, they dove into the cotton and pulled themselves toward the bottom and found the metal mesh that now covered urine-colored dead grass, and then they turned around, pushing upwards, toward the orange light, toward the air.

Peter saw it all. He was squatting behind a row of trees, delicately holding back a ring of thorns. It was almost dark and the world had blurred. He couldn't control his breathing; his undershirt was stuck to his chest; the thorns were pricking into his palms, into his fingers. One scratched his neck like a broken fingernail.

He saw the pickup truck, almost gray and invisible in the dusk, slowly creeping down the dirty road toward the bins. It was already almost a hundred yards away.

Peter had summoned it. He had seen the 4Runner on his initial drive by the field, and in silence, with no thinking, no pause to consider what he was doing, he drove around the circumference of the field, looking for the nearest one-story farmer's house, trying to find the one with that truck. It didn't take long. The truck was innocently parked in a carport, and Peter idled in front of the house, leaning on the horn, until a curtain twitched in one of the windows and he was sure he had been seen. He then stomped on the accelerator and sped back to the cotton bins.

Lina's dark green SUV floated next to the bins like a fat shadow. They continued to dive—an awkward and sincere motion. Peter heard Lina giggle. A cell phone chirped from inside the 4Runner, but it was ignored. Their clothing lay strewn on the lip of the bin. A couple of articles rested on the top of the 4Runner. Jeremy was a pale shadow, with dirty shadings where his hair was supposed to be. Lina was compact and dark. The belly-necklace sparkled. The sky behind the bins had turned a navy blue.

Peter heard a twig snap under the tire of the approaching truck.

He thrashed, twisting his body. A thorn traced across his forearm, and he felt a sizzling sting. It left a thin, red scratch— the kind that never bleeds but always appears to be on the cusp of bleeding. Lina and Jeremy continued to dive. He saw them perform a flip into a bin together, hollering as they dove. Peter could almost see the recoil of the cotton as it caught them.

The truck was fifty feet away. Peter saw the vague outline of a driver bent over the wheel.

Peter sucked his scratch, hoping to make the sting go away. Lina and Jeremy did not come up from the cotton. He knew they were under its covers now. He fought the urge to run for the bins and fling himself into the cotton. Instead, he turned around and walked back to his car, sloppily parked in the soybean field behind the trees. He left the couple naked in the cotton, floating together in the twilight with the pickup truck approaching. He left them to go home, back to his mother who would be waiting at the dinner table with her old man.

ॐ

Peter did not hear from Jeremy for another week. Both he and Lina were at school but neither approached him. He didn't even see them together. All he got as he walked down the hall was a fake, partial smile, or a slight head nod. After a week, Jeremy finally approached Peter after school.

"Hey, man."

Peter was leaning over his backpack, trying to force the zipper to close.

"Ya think we could start carpooling again?" Jeremy asked.

Without looking up Peter said sure.

They walked out to the parking lot. The dark blue Lincoln sat alone. Frost had hit and they moved slowly in their thick jackets and under their bulging backpacks. When they had almost reached the car, Jeremy said, "Hey, Peter. I'm sorry about the last week. About not talking. I've been in some serious shit."

Peter nodded, said yeah, he'd heard things.

They crawled into the car. The doors whined. Peter put the heater on high but the air was cold at first. The seats and steering wheel felt stale.

Once they were situated, the backpacks put away, the wipers massaging the blurry windshield, the boys buckled in and rubbing their hands together, Jeremy looked over at Peter with a frightened but elated smile. "Pete. Man, I have had the weirdest fucking week. You wouldn't believe it. You wouldn't believe what happened to Lina and me. We—"

"Get out," Peter said, his hands now stuffed into his coat pockets. The smile on Jeremy's face made Peter want to pummel him.

"What?"

"Get the fuck out."

"Pete, I—"

"I said get the fuck out of my car."

"Man, I'm sor—"

"Jeremy Moultas, if you don't get out of my car right now, I'm gonna beat the shit out of you."

Peter was now shaking, and his fists coiled around Jeremy's undershirt, just below the soft, hollow indention of his throat. He yanked him close enough to see the darkness of his mouth, to feel his breath, the only warm substance in the car. In his grip there was a tear—perhaps only a stitch—that sounded to Peter like a distant explosion from somewhere deep inside Jeremy.

"I'm so not kidding, J."

Jeremy grabbed his things and fled the car, and Peter sped away.

ᑕᔑ

With no explanation to his mother, Peter insisted shortly thereafter that the family sell the Lincoln Town Car. His parents were mystified, but Peter staunchly refused to drive it ever again, and after two weeks of acquiescing to his mother's pleading ("I just don't have time to take you to school every morning"), he dropped the keys on the kitchen counter and did not come near the car for the six more weeks it took them to sell it. Everyone tried to talk sense into him, even his grandfather. That's a perfectly good car, he had said. It was good enough for *me*. Everyone thought that Peter was embarrassed about the car's model, its angular shape, its bruised color. Listen to me, son, he continued, keep driving that car. I'll buy you a new one as soon as you get into college. Grandpa pushed his glasses up on top of his bald head, a gesture known throughout the family as one of concrete sincerity. Son, he finished, it ain't a bad car. I know it ain't *cool*. And then, pulling Peter closer, he said: Son, listen, I promise you that car'll get you pussy just as fast as anything else.

Timber Walking

"The splitter—sucks for you," said Tubbel.

"You on delivery still?" asked Peter.

"You know it," Tubbel said, spitting out chewed-up halves of sunflower seeds. They caught in the wind, flew, and then crashed onto his jacket sleeve.

"You know," said Tubbel, "I just don't know what this has got to do with baseball."

Peter heard his father calling his name from their splitter. He stepped down off the log with a heavy adolescent sigh, positioned his baseball hat just so, and walked back to work.

 G3

Since the beginning of the project, Peter had spent most of his time with his father and Nikolai. He and his father had worked delivery the first couple of weekends, but his father disliked it. Peter thought that the process was too volatile for him: piling the wood into the trailer, taking it off to a house in a subdivision outside of town, stacking the wood in its selected spot, and driving back to the farm to repeat everything. He needed a quieter repetition. Sometimes the customers would invite them in for hot chocolate. The families were usually other parents from school. Peter and his father were polite and always came in for a few minutes, taking off their muddy shoes at the doorway and sliding around the kitchen island in their sock feet with their canvas work gloves in one hand and a warm, steaming mug in the other. Peter would push his hat back on the top of his head and look around at the kitchen, smelling the food everywhere. He couldn't see it but thought he could find it, given the time. His father never stayed long. He usually gulped down his cup quickly as if he were afraid the coldness that hung about him all day would evaporate quickly once inside. So they would leave soon and head back to the farm to take another load.

Nikolai was Siberian, a thick-chested man who was a little shorter than Peter's father and spoke English slowly and deliberately. He was built like a brick shithouse, in the terminology of Peter's grandfather. He had red hair and a constant grin on his face as he wrapped his thick arms around three-foot-long sections of tree trunk. He would grab them from their bed of sawdust and place them with a thud next to the splitter. A tuft of red chest hair always poked out of the top of his flannel shirt, as if the hair were attempting to force the shirt open. Nikolai always had sawdust in his hair, on his chest, in his beard, and on his arms, and he was always giving Peter and his father his hearty, sweaty smile and a thick jab to the shoulder, which always knocked Peter off balance. The three worked together and always got the horizontal splitter, the one where you laid the log down, pressed the button, and the iron spade came sputtering down toward the log and split it, the wood crying under the stress and sapwater sometimes coming out of the cracks, as if deep inside the log there were tiny, invisible pools. They would start with Nikolai's big log, split it in two, then split those halves again, and then those new ones again. They laid them in a pile for the boys working delivery.

Peter was fourteen when he and his father split wood out at the Dickerson Stables, raising money for their baseball team's spring break trip. *This trip is going to be the chance of a baseball lifetime*, the coach had said. A tornado had come the first weekend in October and dug a scar along the northeast side of Jackson like a boot through mud. The area just north of the Dickerson Stables had received the worst damage—it was now a wasteland of timber. A week after the storm the coach had struck some sort of deal with the Dickersons and there they were.

It was a damp autumn, and they arrived every Saturday and Sunday by 7 a.m., the hydraulic splitters already in place, gargling awake like green, steel animals. The sawdust from the last weekend's work would lie wet in tan mounds next to the crippled and dismembered oak, pine, and cedar trees. The Mexicans, who were chainsawing the trees into manageable sections, were always already at work.

ɔ

In the spring, junior varsity practice was every Wednesday afternoon. Peter played third base, and he spent the first half of practice taking ground balls. The coach would stand in the batter's box with his fungo bat and "shape" the boys up. That's what he called it. "I'm gonna shape you boys up!" And then he would start at third, the first ground ball in his whole routine, the peak of his energy. After he got through with the infield, he would stop to talk, pointing his critiques to each boy with his skinny, aluminum bat. He would end the sermon by striking home plate. The sound was a combination of the rubber thud of the home plate and the muted ring of the aluminum bat. It wasn't that loud compared to his yelling, but everyone heard it.

Peter's father always came out Wednesdays. He stood high in the bleachers next to third base, his suit coat gently folded next to him, a cloud of cigarette smoke slowly dissolving around his head. Peter thought he looked thirty feet tall from where he was, gleaming in his crisp white shirt, his shining silk tie. He looked so peaceful, so contemplative, with his arms folded over his chest. Peter tried to ignore his father and pay attention to the coach who pointed at him intermittently. When the coach tossed the ball up in the air, it seemed to levitate for a frozen moment, and Peter thought that he could stop everything in that moment, that he could put the practice on pause, fixing the coach in mid-swing, and that he could quietly, calmly lay down his glove on the lip of the infield, walk over to the bleachers, and bum a cigarette from his father. But this vision was always interrupted by the same aluminum ping, followed by the same dusty fumbling, then the slinging of the ball to Tubbel, who leaned out from first, spitting sunflower seeds upwind.

Each day this vision extended, lengthened, and the aluminum shattering grew more painful. During practice, in these moments of fugue-like languor, his mind floated above the drills, and he looked down upon the field and his position, upon his point in the geometry of adolescence. But always the ball—like some unnamable, tightly wound dread—came suddenly upon him and forced him back into himself.

After every throw he would remain crouched over with his hand in the dirt, momentarily spent. He would spit out the dust and stand back up for the next play, assume the ready position, and no matter how good or bad the throw, he always thought, *Don't look to the bleachers.*

℞

They broke for lunch at around 12:30. To keep himself full through the morning, Peter would visit the water cooler every fifteen minutes or so. As they unpacked their brown paper bags, Peter and his father sat on the stumps and looked back over the fallen trees and the other players and fathers spread throughout the remains of the forest—a gray haze, the ground littered with bark and sawdust. Some brought gloves to throw after lunch but Peter always said it was too cold. Nikolai was on a stump next to them eating a sandwich and smiling whenever they looked over at him. Peter's father had a routine of lunchtime questions.

"Nikolai, what do you think about here?" He always spoke to him loudly and deliberately. "Do you like working with all us baseball players?" His father smiled and tussled Peter's hair. Peter was staring into the ground and breathing into his sandwich, held close to his lips.

"Is good work." Nikolai smiled over his roast beef. "I work in labs all day, every day. It feels good to be out with these boys. I ... don't know baseball, never seen them play, but their face," and he touched his right hand to his red, smiling cheek, "I see promise."

"Yeah, these are good boys," his father said. Peter realized he was holding him by the shoulder and looking at him, and Peter smiled quickly. They finished the rest of their lunches without talking and went back to work.

☃

One early Saturday evening during that same autumn, Peter walked through the house trying to find his father. He wanted to talk to him about next season, how he had been thinking a lot lately about folding up his glove on the lip of the infield. It was late October, and they had been working out at the stables for a couple of weeks. Peter had already taken a shower and was waiting around for dinner. The smell of cooking in the kitchen made him lose his patience, so he began to walk around the house. He walked up the stairs and heard the water running in the bathroom at the end of the hall. He approached the open door and saw his father standing in front of the mirror, looking at himself, only in his sweat pants, his bare belly a proud globe. His white feet stuck out at the bottom, wet and speckled with bits of dirt and leaves; his chest was wet, and the black hair that covered it was stuck together in a hundred tiny waves; his hands were stained brown halfway up his forearm, tanned and muddied from pushing his sleeves up; his face looked tired but calm, and he pushed his hands through his hair, as if wiping them off.

Peter's father looked in the mirror for a moment longer and then lifted his left arm into the air above his head and nuzzled his nose down into his armpit and took in a deep breath. His chest swelled and Peter could see his ribs poke out beneath the white skin and the black, wet hair. Peter stepped backwards and stumbled into the banister. His father exhaled and without turning to him said, "Whatcha need, bud?"

"Nothing. I think that dinner is going to be ready soon," Peter said.

"Okay." He smiled, and Peter identified this as his regular smile: slightly sleepy, no teeth showing, a bemused hint of a smirk, a genuine indication of good spirits. "Tell Mom I'll be down after my shower." Peter turned away and heard his father close the bathroom door gently.

03

They continued to split wood on into the afternoon. Every hour or so Tubbel would appear with one of the other players and pile the wood into the trailer, constantly talking about the last house they visited, where it was, how nice the family was. Nikolai, Peter, and his father looked up at Tubbel from the splitter, but never talked over the crunching and cracking. They kept on piling timber, splitting it again and again with Peter at the controls, situating each log and smacking the button. Peter and his father grasped the sections as the spade divided them and then put back the new piece. When Peter hit the button, the splitter groaned, hissed, and a thin, peeling chorus filled the air. Nikolai kept the timber coming steadily, walking from the nearest cut tree with two gigantic slices of trunk, one on each shoulder. Peter felt the thud run through the earth when Nikolai placed them on the ground between his father and the splitter. They felt like the sock-footed steps of some giant. And Nikolai, walking back for more, started singing, giving them a rhythm and a melody for work. Nikolai had said that singing and working made each stronger, and he sang a proud, endless melody in Russian. The only thing to be heard from their part of the flattened forest was the groan of the splitter and the cadence of Nikolai's voice.

Nikolai was walking down the length of a fallen tree to retrieve the cut-up sections, placing one foot in front of the other, swaying in time with his voice.

"Nikolai, what in the hell are you doing?" asked his father. Nikolai stood on the fallen tree with two huge sections of timber on his shoulders. Peter's father leaned onto the splitter happily. His hat was pushed up, his forehead shining in sweat.

"I'm ... timber walking," Nikolai said with a broad smile. "Couldn't you tell?" Nikolai and Peter's father hooted together. Peter was gathering the newly divided wood and stopped to watch them, Nikolai erupting back into song, and his father trying to join him, trying to follow the melody and mimicking every third word or so. Peter put the wood into its pile and continued silently.

Peter began to find a rhythm in their singing. He would place the wood, then hit the button, wait for the groaning of the splitter to stop, hit the button again, and retrieve the split timber. He did this over and over. Place the wood, hit the button; the wood groans, maybe cries sap; hit the button, grab the wood, repeat. Place, hit, groan, hit, grab, repeat. Then, he heard his father's voice, politely quiet at first.

"Peter. Stop it, Peter. Stop the goddamn machine. Peter, my finger, Peter."

His father had caught his finger in one of the cracks in the log. As the splitter came down the log, making a scar longer and deeper, all those other cracks and crevices sealed under the pressure. His father had the thumb of his right hand caught in a crack, which grew tighter each moment. His father gradually screamed, and Nikolai immediately stopped singing and threw down his logs and ran over. Peter could not immediately comprehend the image in front of him—his father yelling and twisting up on his toes, Nikolai running down the log, the metal spade plowing forward. Peter hit the button. The splitter stopped. His father's thumb was still caught in the log. Nikolai jumped next to his father and grabbed the log with his two gloved hands and began to stick his fingers down next to the trapped thumb, attempting to pry open the log. Peter stood there and watched as his father let out a high-pitched, quiet squeal. Nikolai groaned, a phlegmatic sound, and the log began to squeak and split. Nikolai's forehead became red as his hair and veins flexed out below his hairline, and with one final grunt and gasp the log broke, a fourth of it flying to the ground. Peter's father was freed and fell backwards to the ground and Nikolai tripped over his feet and fell on top of him. There was a tossing of leaves and bark as Nikolai yelled, "Lemmee see! Lemmee see!"

Nikolai examined the gloved hand. He pulled the ripped leather off gently, and then Peter saw the pink thumb of his father, shaking and uninjured. Both men sighed and fell back on one another. There was a nervous chuckle and then a kind of silence—only the soft droning of the other splitters in the distance.

Peter saw them lying there, and he looked again at the healthy thumb and projected into the future: he saw his father at his desk on Monday morning, picking up his phone to talk with four fingers and a vacant stub; he saw his father washing his face in the sink, one hand unable to grip the slippery soap; he saw his father at practice up in the stands, learning to flick his cigarette with his left hand; he saw his father picking up the baseball out of the infield dirt, rolling it around over his four fingers and his palm, and trying to explain to him how a curve-ball was supposed to be thrown—what it was *supposed* to look like. Peter saw all of these things in his mind, and he began to run. But there were logs everywhere, stumps like landmines, and he tripped and fell, burying himself in a tan cloud of sawdust. A chorus of apologies repeated in his head as the sawdust and wood shavings crowded his neck and face. He did not consider getting up.

It felt like a very long time before his father came over to him and pulled him up out of the sawdust, hooking his hands under Peter's armpits and lifting. He stood in front of his father, still covered in bits and pieces of wood, coughing dust and apologizing quietly and continuously. He couldn't seem to stop crying. He saw that his father was proudly filthy, his Niskayuna High sweatshirt spotted with mud.

"It's okay, son. It's okay. I'm okay, bud. Don't apologize." As he said this, his father began to wipe Peter off, rubbing his shoulders and patting down his back. He brushed off the sawdust, the bits of bark and leaves, and the clumps of mud, speaking warmly, almost humming, "It's okay. It's okay."

Peter closed his eyes. The sawdust floated towards the ground. His father was now rubbing across his shoulders and down in between his shoulder blades. Peter's head tipped forward. His father began on the back of his neck, standing above his son, nearly eight inches taller. Peter felt his father's breath. He opened his eyes and saw the white puff of his father's breath pulsing down around his face, as his father continued to brush off his sweatshirt. Nikolai stood in front of him, his smile a muscular reflex, neck and lips and scalp shining red and pulsing with his breath. Peter listened to them both, the way the rush of their breath slowed, how they were both gradually leveling out, and he watched their two brief white clouds mix and disappear, mix and disappear, and he could see and feel the steam coming off them, like the extra energy was melting in that cold.

It was then that Peter decided he would quit baseball, that the idea of spending another spring buried in that dugout was somehow intolerable, that his secret was now somehow safe to recognize, safe to release. But in the wet silence of that Mississippi November, he knew he wouldn't tell his father yet— couldn't—until all the timber was gone. There must be limits to cruelty, Peter thought. He slid out from under his father's hand and walked back to the splitter and the waiting timber.

Nightswimming

She had called.

It was the night before the first day of senior year, a Sunday, a day normally reserved for lunch with the grandparents, minimal yard work for his mother, and an evening spent grilling hotdogs with his father in the driveway of his Belhaven rental, where he had lived since the trial separation began. But tonight was different. He had begged off their weekly cookout because of school. All that prep for the big first day, he'd said. He had been idly flipping through the channels, bored and a little hot in his upstairs room, and then the phone call finally came—special dispensation.

Peter walked downstairs to his mother's bedroom, rubbed his eyes, and knocked gently. His eyebrows were bent into inquisitive blond arches.

"What do you want now?" his mother asked. She was watching television in her chair, her leg draped over one arm, gently kicking the air. She was smiling at whatever was on.

"Becca asked me to come over and watch a movie."

"A movie?"

"Yeah."

"Why would you want to go over there to see a movie?"

"You know, just ... because."

"Oh. Be*cause*."

"Yeah."

"On a school night?"

"*Mom.*"

She cackled and finally broke off her stare from the television. "Be home early."

"I will."

"And be sweet."

"Be sweet" was his mother's euphemism for everything, what she always told Peter before he left the house. Peter had come to understand this over the years. It meant: do things that would keep him sweet, or do not do things that wouldn't.

Peter left his mother and stomped up the stairs, a loud march. He went to his dresser, found the box in which his dress watch had come (a gift from two birthdays before). He gently untied the box and lifted the lid. The silver band shone in the dim light of his bedroom; he had only worn it three, perhaps four, times in the past two years. He lifted the stiff circular collar that the watch rested upon, underneath which was his stash of condoms, blue Trojans, spermicidally lubricated. He tucked a single condom into the special "condom pocket" of his khaki shorts.

Peter thought that his Gap brand khaki shorts were truly unique. There was a pocket on the right side of the chino situated between the regular-sized pocket and the zipper, closer to the hip in distance and possibly a descendent of the watch pocket, the appearance of which in some pants and most jeans had always puzzled and bothered Peter until he entered high school. This pocket was ideal for storing a single condom. There the condom was protected from the elements, the pressure of a hot, leather wallet, the sitting pressure of the body. The condom was also easily and constantly accessible and yet inconspicuous. All of this pleased Peter immensely.

As he machine-gunned downstairs and swung open the backdoor, he thought of his mother sitting alone at the end of the hall in her room, saw the amber glow emanating from the half-open doorway where the TV laughed.

"Hey, Mom. About to go. Thanks again for the dinner."

"... welcome, Peter ..." was all he could make out. Earlier, happy he was home for a Sunday evening and for once not off being "indoctrinated" by his father, she had made Chicken Spaghetti, known throughout the family as one of his favorites.

Peter wasn't especially sophisticated but he knew that each time he ate the meal, he was fulfilling the second half of a sentimental gesture. He wanted to say something more, to be more emphatic in his gratitude. But he was already running late.

ೞ

As far as Peter knew, Becca's parents never left her alone longer than it took her mother to venture to the grocery store one afternoon a week, usually a Tuesday. Their dates, crowded with friends and school-related functions, did not lend themselves to intimacy. Her house was bright, large, open-doored and always chaperoned. On those Tuesdays the summer before, Becca and Peter would go swimming out back in her pool and would wrestle around in the deep end, under the water. They would kiss down near the concrete floor, legs and fingers interlocking, a bikini pretzel. These water maneuvers would only last an hour or so, until Mrs. Cartright's permed head could be seen bopping around the kitchen or the living room of the house. Afterwards, they swam slowly. They were quiet, tired, and frustrated.

The drive to her house took seven minutes in regular traffic, accounting for the average number of stops by traffic lights. But Peter was determined to make it in five tonight and green lights glowed in the distance.

CB

Becca didn't have a movie. She and Peter curled up under a blanket and flipped channels. She ate popcorn, greasy and sticky with butter. Peter refrained from snacking, said he was too full from dinner. When he held her hand, the fingertips were moist, slippery. When they kissed, her lips tasted like salt and butter mixed. But mostly their faces were drawn to the TV and they spoke only sideways, during visual lulls.

"So who died?" Peter asked.

"Uhm ... one of my cousin's sons, I think. I don't really know."

"Sad."

"They said I didn't have to go, since I didn't really know him."

"I'm sorry about that."

"Oh, it's okay. My parents are all right with it."

"They were cool with letting you stay alone?"

"Yeah. Completely. I mean, they're going to be back by like four tomorrow. So it isn't that bad."

"Mmm."

"Did your mom say anything when you asked to come over?" Becca asked.

"No. She was cool."

"Really?"

"Yeah ..." he said, turning to face her, and fighting the vague desire to shrug, "you know."

This meant that yes, she was fine; she had given permission and that meant she was fine. Peter did not want to think about the possibility of his mother saying one thing but secretly wanting something else.

"What's she doing?"

"The usual."

The night was warm and the door to the room was open and the wind blew in from the balcony. When Becca wasn't looking, Peter glanced at her face. He could see the reflection of the television in her eyes. They were pale blue, and Peter thought they shined, though he couldn't decide how much of this blueness came from the TV. He watched her eyelashes wave and close and open. They were so long, like filaments or whiskers. They looked like those bright floating strands that lived on coral, undulating near the ocean floor.

A commercial for a water park came on the television.

"God, I haven't been to one of those in years," said Becca. She smelled of butter and sweat, and there was the intermittent aroma of soapy lavender coming from her bathroom. He'd always specifically loved her bathroom.

"I used to go all the time when I was like nine or so," he said.

"Really?"

"Yeah. Like three days a week."

"Did you actually get tan?" Becca asked.

"Very funny."

"Tanning's overrated anyway," she said.

"I used to really like it. I would just float out in the wave pool for hours."

"Were you checking out the chicks?"

"I was, like, nine."

"So?"

"Well, I wasn't like hitting on them or anything. I was just floating around."

"Oh. I see. Perv."

Peter smirked, a sarcasm deflector.

"But there was this one completely beautiful lifeguard there," he said.

"You slut. What was her name?"

"I don't know."

"You never got her name?"

"I was, like, nine."

"Yeah. Anyway. Continue. What about her?"

"Well, she was just really pretty. Only, I couldn't see her face all that well. She was so high up in that chair in all that sun. But I used to look at her when I was floating on one of those rafts—you know the ones you rent?"

"Yeah."

"I would watch her when the waves shut off."

"Did she ever see you?"

"No, I don't think so."

"Too bad."

"Yeah, I guess."

Becca's hand went for more popcorn.

"I did think about getting her attention somehow," Peter said.

"Yeah?"

"Well. I thought: she's a lifeguard. She has to guard my life. So I often thought of just slipping off my raft whenever the waves turned back on, and seeing if she would come get me."

"No."

"Yeah."

"Do you think she would've?"

"Of course she would've. It was her job."

"Yeah. But—"

"I had already seen her save a fat kid earlier that summer. And he was twice as big as me. Why wouldn't she have saved me?"

"How did she do it?"

"Save him?"

"Yeah."

"With that red foam-thing. You know, their special life preserver. It looks like a finger."

"Or a tongue."

"Do you know what I'm talking about?"

"Yeah, I know. Those things are so damn cool."

"Yeah."

Peter was excited and tried to look back at the television.

"Hey, Peter."

Silence. He was trying not to stare at her. She's scheming, he thought.

"What?"

"Do you know what we should do?"

"What?"

"Go nightswimming."

"What?"

"Nightswimming. You ever been?"

"No." Peter stared into the shallow mound of the popcorn.

"Peter," she said, touching his fingers just above the bowl and holding him with her eyes, "it's way fun."

ༀ

"Son, you should know that what you're about to enter is an exciting time. I don't have to tell you this. You're about to piss yourself as it is, I can tell. You're already excited about everything. And I want you to be. I don't want you to let what's going on between your Mom and me get in the way of you enjoying yourself for these next few years. We're all going to work it out and whatever happens, you know that I love you and that's what's important. I'll still be there for you. And I'm going to try not to be jealous or live through you in some way like some fathers do. But I have to admit that the next few years will probably be the best years of your life. You probably have no idea what I'm talking about. That's okay. Youth's wasted on the young, anyway. But I want you to remember, want you to remember what I'm about to say: What you're about to go through will never be repeated. Remember that. It's precious and brief and it only happens once.

"We'll get that new car pretty soon and you probably won't listen to a word I say afterwards. It's okay. It's to be expected. I don't know where you are, so to speak, but sooner or later, you'll only smell gasoline and pussy, and anything me or your mother says won't really compare to those two smells. And I'm not going to tell you to hold it in, son. Your Mom might, but I won't lie to you: some of the best pussy I ever got was when I was in high school, so I'm not about to pretend that you won't be involved. But I would tell you to take it slow. Slow Down. Don't be in such a rush to grow up. Get laid. Get a job. Whatever. But remember to be a kid for a while.

"But if you do, for God's sake use a condom. I'm not going to try to twist your arm and go for the abstinence route because basically I think it's a bunch of bullshit. Men and women were built for fucking and anyone trying to pretend it doesn't happen is deluded. But I would caution you to use a condom. There is a lot of frightening shit out there and just because you're with the preps at Niskayuna doesn't mean it can't get you.

"And to be completely honest, it's not the VDs I'm all that worried about. I mean, the sweetest looking girl in your class could be a landmine of viruses and she would still be the captain of the cheerleading squad and the softest cupcake this side of town. But more than that use the condom to prevent pregnancy. Don't believe they're on the pill. They might say they're on the pill and they might in fact *be* on the pill but for God's sake don't trust them that they're on the pill. I know you might be in love and that's great. Love is great. I would caution you to take it slow and to play the field but in general love is great, but still don't trust her to take the pill. Put a fucking rubber on your dick. It is the most important thing you can do. Because son, I love you, but you haven't the slightest clue how much an unwanted pregnancy can fuck your entire life prospects. None of the options are good, and I know you want to go to college, find a career, do something with your life. Whatever. But trust me, if you get Stacy or Tracy or what's-her-name pregnant, you're going to be up shit creek and you will be tied to that woman and that child for the rest of your life. I know you have no idea of the magnitude of that but trust me that you end up living a hell of a long time.

"And I'll let you in on a little secret, too. A single white man is the freest thing on this earth. If you can manage to get out of college and still be single and to keep yourself clean, you will have more freedom than practically anyone. But if you get someone pregnant, you've just used your dick to sign a contract it'll take the rest of your life to pay off.

"I'm not telling you all this to scare you. I'm just trying to share some advice. Things I wish I knew when I was your age. All of this will probably not mean a thing to you. But it makes me feel better just to say it. The next ten years will be the best ten years of your life, probably. I wish I could make you see that."

☙

Peter stood out near the pool in his swimming trunks, the special yellow pair that Becca kept for him in her room for those spontaneous summer swims. Becca wore a red bikini. She flipped the switch for the pool lights. They flickered and went out. Peter stood with his toes hanging over the side of the pool, looking down into the dark water.

"Ah. It's okay. I like the dark," he said. He dove in and turned around. All he could see was the glow of red slowly coming toward him.

They swam for a long time, diving off the board and splashing tremendous waves, bubbles and foam exploding to the sky. They pulled each other down to the bottom, kissing and wrapping around each other and waiting as long as they could, twisted together like a knot of flesh, until they could control their bodies no longer and had to rush to the surface and fling their heads upward, gasping for air. They stood there inhaling deeply and violently. Water droplets fell in sparkles from her eyelashes. He reached his hand over and touched her face—the way you might touch a painting, gently, as not to get caught or set off alarms, only using enough pressure to feel the texture of the artifact. He kissed her and tasted the salt from the popcorn still on her lips. She kissed his cheeks where the water trickled down like tears. Later, they took turns doing cannonballs and jackknifes, but they always ended up stuck together, revolving around each other, sinking toward the bottom.

After a while, Becca looked up to the balcony just outside the television room.

"Hey Peter, want to make a bigger splash?" She was whispering. They were folded together.

He turned to the balcony overlooking the pool. The black iron in the darkness made it and its spiral staircase look like a shadow. But Peter was so eager, he did not even turn to agree to Becca's suggestion.

They walked up the stairs, leaving a trail of wet footprints across the concrete. Peter looked out over her backyard. The arches of his feet tingled. The tile of the pool deck was traced by grass and then palmetto shrubs; the area was almost hidden, like an oasis-mirage. He felt the wind on his damp back, and his arms turned to gooseflesh.

"Becca?" Peter said.

"Yeah," she said, touching his face.

"Let's do something."

❧

"What do you mean you haven't done it?" asked Anderson.

"What do you mean, 'what do I mean'? I mean, we haven't done it."

"But *why*?"

"Because."

"Because? That's not a good enough reason."

"Well, it's gotta be. What are you, my mother?"

"Please. I would like to know why you've still not nailed the proclaimed Girl of Your Dreams, one Miss Becca Cartright."

"Hey, I'm not 'nailing' anyone. She's not a tree. Don't make it sound so crass."

"Oh, God. Stop being sensitive. You're always so fucking po*lite*."

"As opposed to you."

"Yes, as opposed to me. I at least have ..."

"Don't even try that. You haven't done it either."

"Well, at least I've gotten to third base—"

"With a girl who later puked into a planter. Yes, Anderson, that *is* something to be proud of."

"Shut up."

"Look, don't get offended. She *did* get sick shortly after ..."

"I said *shut up.*"

"Fine."

"At least I've done *some*thing. At least I've tried."

"That's not fair. I want to try. I just want it to be ... you know, right."

"'Right'? What are you doing, directing a movie? Just fuck her. You want to. She wants to. This isn't a quadratic equation. Willing plus Able equals Fuck Buddies, *comprende*? I mean, you've been going out for *nine months.* What are you waiting for, a blessing?"

ଔ

In anticipation of what he hoped was a romantic inevitability, Peter often practiced putting on a condom. He knew this inevitability would be with Becca, was sure it would be with Becca, was almost 100 percent positive it would be with Becca. He had definite notions about the importance of love in the carnal transaction, the "prerequisite" of love, he thought of it, after learning that word from college admissions material. In fact, all these idealistic notions had been strengthened rather than broken by the marital fluctuations of his parents and the parents of everyone else he knew. But he was terrified of not using the condom right, of the situation arising and there being much fumbling and tearing and blind groping—basically the worst kind of pin-the-tail-on-the-donkey game ever.

The paranoia regarding the condoms in part sprung from a ninth grade sexual education class, where Dr. Roman gave a lecturette entitled "The Importance of Masturbation and Prophylactic Practice in Adolescent Males." The title alone made the room full of boys turn crimson, slide their feet, wipe their hands on their jeans. Roman maintained that not only should boys masturbate to "gain self-knowledge" but they should also rehearse the actual administration of the birth control device. Roman demonstrated the proper technique with a banana.

Consequently, there were occasions when Peter would stand in front of his wall-length bathroom mirror, naked, and would practice administering the condom on himself. He was always struck by the smell—metallic, antiseptic—the concept of "lubrication" and the unexpected coldness. Roman had said that the condom came out of the wrapper like a miniature derby, "or like a latex yarmulke for all our non-Christian students," and that if one attempted to "put the hat on backwards," the condom was effectively ruined. Because of this, Peter was deliberate and kept all of the lights on. He thought that he should have this procedure down the same way he should have driving a standard transmission down, an initially awkward physical task that could be mastered to the point of becoming second nature. But all he could think once he was readied and was analyzing his appearance in the mirror was that he hoped that whenever the time came, the area in which the event occurred was extremely dark.

೦೪

Not pausing to reflect further, his presence on the metal balcony like an out-of-body experience, Peter pulled the drawstring of his swimming trunks ever so slowly and let them fall to his ankles. He stepped out of them and tossed them over the side of the balcony with his foot. They landed with a loud, wet clap on the concrete next to the pool. Her eyes seemed to glow by themselves in the darkness, and Peter thought it was magical. Peter climbed over the rail and stood at the edge of the balcony, holding his hand out, balancing. He turned to the pool below. It was completely dark, as if it wasn't even there. Peter took a deep breath, his lungs filled with the aroma of chlorine, and he was positive it was still down there, ready to catch him. He dove twenty feet into the water. He broke the surface with a quick splash, touched the rough floor of the pool, and turned.

His face bobbed to the surface, hair mussed, giggles tossed back up to Becca. She stood above, holding the railing of the balcony.

"So are you going to join me?" he asked.

She smiled at him and climbed over the rail of the balcony. She leaned back against the rail and unhooked her bikini top and let it float down to the water. She then carefully stepped out of her bikini bottoms, first the left foot, then the right, the material rolling into a twisted rubber band. She let the bottoms fall into the water and a moment later she was falling after them, her empty hands making small circular motions on the way down as if she were perhaps trying to fly.

They clutched on the surface and twisted down to the bottom. They intertwined their legs, arms, fingers. Peter looked into her eyes, the only things he could see; the rest had disappeared. They were so close he felt her everywhere. And his mind raced—popcorn, television, car, Mom, chicken spaghetti, the image of his father eating alone, Anderson ecstatically smoking a cigarette just after school, the word *virgin*—the pictures all came rushing forth so uncontrolled, so unexpected, and Becca was holding him, about to slide him into place, and at that moment he pictured his shorts, tossed over the arm of a recliner in Becca's living room, the content of the secret pocket barely visible as a small, elevated ring. Peter panicked, recoiled, and blurted out her name. The water filled his open mouth.

He broke the surface gagging and coughing and trying desperately to breathe. Becca wrapped her arms around him and guided him to the edge of the pool and called out his name, over and over. Peter jerked and waved his arms around as if he were losing balance and had something stuck deep down inside his chest. Becca would not let go of him.

"Peter, I'm sorry. I'm so sorry. You're okay. You're okay. Just let it out. You're safe in the air now."

Finally, Peter gargled once very deeply and vomited. He continued coughing and spitting and gasping for air through it all, and Becca kept talking quietly to him and running her hand through his hair and holding his chest with the other. He held onto the side of the pool and the rail of the ladder and could almost stand. Just then, as Peter started to catch his breath and started to taste the sour mucus in his mouth, the lights to the pool flickered on, and a phosphorescence glowed under them. It was then that Peter saw his vomit floating in the water next to him, identifiable bits of noodle, and he saw it on his body, on Becca's arm wrapped tightly around his chest.

She washed him off in her parents' shower stall, a huge tile cell. Peter could not hear himself crying over the pulse of the water. When he opened his eyes, he saw Becca with soapy hands and arms, scrubbing him down, the pink tips of her bare breasts slightly swaying.

He stopped crying and she dried him off. She was still wet, beads of water standing guard on her back, and she knelt down and dried his shins and feet. When he began to talk again, he kept repeating, "I'm so late. She's gonna flip out. She's gonna fucking flip." Becca just nodded and went to retrieve his shirt and his shoes, his socks stuffed inside, and his shorts, still thrown over the armrest of the recliner. When he got dressed, Becca walked him to her front door. She was still undressed, undried even from the pool and then the shower. However, she had washed off all the signs of his nausea, and he realized this was the first time he had seen her naked.

Though the porch light was on and the front entrance to her house was fully visible to the road, Becca opened the door to let Peter leave. She did not speak, and she did not flinch. Peter shrank from the glaring light and turned back to her, and she stepped aside and flipped a switch and the porch turned to darkness. This seemed to relieve some accumulating stress. Peter tried to mimic her calmness, though when he turned around to kiss her goodnight, her large eyes seemed darker, more opaque, as if considering him from a distance. He knew he had to go; he was sure that each minute made his potential violation worse, but he felt that he had to explain himself in some way. She gave him more than enough room to speak.

"Do you wanna stay?" she asked.

"Better not," he said.

He didn't want to look her in the eyes, but felt guilty for staring at her body instead. In the end, Peter kissed her dryly and walked quickly to his car.

ఇ

The streets were empty. He drove slowly, hitting every red light, nine minutes into his drive home already and only halfway there. He imagined what he would say to Becca when he called her later, smothered under the sheets of his bed, making his usual post-visit checkup. He wondered what his mother would say when he walked in the door a few minutes later. Would she be sitting on the counter, her hands planted on each side, staring him down and worried? Or would she be bent and sleeping in her chair, the TV loud and the lights ablaze?

He came to the intersection two blocks away from his house, sat in his car at the red light. A squad car tore through the intersection just as the light was changing to green, but then silence. He didn't move. Forward movement felt futile: he was replaying the scene in the adolescent theater of his mind, the celluloid memory already looped and endless. The ache in his stomach was the same ache of dread he felt when his parents clashed and parted, the same ache of deep hunger, and he hated his body for having one visceral reaction to the variety of life's absurdities.

The light changed back to red. Perhaps, he thought, they would be okay, as a couple, as a unit, somehow made stronger.

The light changed back to green. Perhaps this would make them closer, increase the chances of intimacy, a rift that would actually weld them together. The idling hum of the car leveled out, a kind of automotive sigh, and he thought that the engine provided the best soundtrack to his grief that he could imagine—that the sexual tension between him and Becca had been a constant, audible rumble. At least, he said to himself, as the glowing circle of light changed from summer green to October orange, this will never be repeated.

Pater Noster

The funeral was fine, the funeral was fine, the funeral was perfectly fine. After a few hours, the crowd back at the house had finally begun to dissipate, and Peter Traxler's mother announced that she would like to lie down. The nonessential guests took their cue and left, and the essential members of the friends and family dissolved into the other rooms to give the impression of a reverent house.

His mother, Susan Hines Traxler, originally from Memphis, hooked onto Peter's arm the way a bride might be escorted down the aisle as they retreated to her bedroom. The only sound in the house was Uncle Dwight cutting the fat from the ham in the kitchen. The peck and scrape of the oversized serrated knife on the good china traveled through the house and found Peter sitting at the foot of his mother's high bed. She was now under the covers, her knees upbent to create a podium for the newspaper, which she had not yet read. In fact, she had come to lie down specifically to read the obituary in private, in a meditative solitude, had been planning it this way all day, had told Peter about the planning so that he was anxious about it, and anxious about everyone shutting up so she could do it, etc. She had everything ready: the scissors, the glue, the cracked, leather Bible—all by her side.

Peter's legs did not reach the floor from where he was sitting, and he kicked them absently.

"Can I get you anything?" he asked.

She sighed.

"I know he must be hungry," she said, "but Jesus. What I'd like more than anything would be complete and total quiet."

Peter stopped bouncing his legs on the bedskirt. The faint but audible scrape continued its call from the kitchen.

"Maybe he's almost finished," Peter said.

Then, a plate dove into the sink followed by the drench of the faucet. Cabinets began opening themselves, followed by the loose-change jangle of the fridge. His mother turned her head sideways, her ears looking forward. Just as Peter thought the house was settling, a glass something spun and shattered and he heard his uncle say, "Well, shit."

"Get him out," his mother said.

"But Mom."

"Get him out. That's what I want. Your father's dead. That means I don't have to put up with him today."

She didn't look at him as she said this, her head still tilted to the side, her high cheeks tight with fury. Peter touched her knee and hopped down off the bed. He said, *Yes, Mother* to himself, silently.

He walked into the kitchen where Dwight was opening random cabinets and saying he was looking for the broom.

"It's in ..." Peter began, but instead went for it himself. When he returned, Dwight was leaning against the granite-topped island, armed with the silver dustpan.

"I'm so sorry about the pitcher," he said. "I'm not doing so well."

Peter patted him on the shoulder and they began picking up the largest chunks of the pitcher, which had scattered from the nucleus of impact all across the black-tiled floor.

"Don't cut yourself now. That's it. Careful there," Dwight kept saying as he floated overhead. Peter could smell the whiskey on him, the way it mixed with the cigarettes, as if his whole body were fermenting. Peter calculated that he was probably still good enough to drive.

Still in his coat, Peter began sweeping, and Dwight bent over and held the dustpan in place to catch the glittering dust.

"I hope you know," he began, huffing hard, his lips red and puckered. "I hope you know ... how much I loved your Daddy."

Peter internally recoiled at Dwight saying the word "Daddy." In life, Dwight had always referred to Peter's father as Eddie or Mr. Ed. "Daddy" was both too distant and too familiar.

"And I hope you know that ..."

Peter dumped the glass dust into the paper sack.

"... hope you know I'll always be here—there—for you. You and your Mama. You know? You know what I'm saying, Pete?"

"Hold it. Lemme get this last bit." Peter took the dustpan from him and swept the thin lines of glass into the pan, delicate like a jeweler. He hated being called Pete.

"I mean, I'll always be here for you. I know we don't live that close and all, but ..."

Peter dumped the last of it, another shower of noise traveling back to the bedroom. There was still a bit of dust left, and Peter could see the faintest glimmer of light in it. He imagined his mother gliding to the fridge in the morning, awakened by grief, and her bare feet sliding into it. He had to get rid of Dwight.

"I mean, do you get what I'm saying, my boy? How I'm here for you and your mother now?"

He had to get rid of Dwight so that he could dampen a hand towel and get on his knees and do it right.

Peter shook the pan in the bag and stood up. Dwight's eyes were watery and Peter looked away. The only sound in the room now was Dwight's noisy breathing.

"I know I can come to you if I need to," Peter said to the sink.

"Do you think your Mama knows?"

"Of course she knows. I'm sure she does."

"I think I would like to talk to her, just for a minute. I've got some things."

"I'm positive she does. Really, Uncle Dwight. She even said how good it was to have you here, this morning."

"I really wanna—"

"She's so tired, Uncle Dwight. And I am, too. And you look tired. Don't you want to go back to the hotel and take a nap?"

"I want to stay here. I want to be around. If somebody needs me. I haven't really gotten to talk any with your mother yet."

Peter scratched his face. His hands still smelled of this morning's cigarette.

"I really think you look like you could use some rest," Peter said. "You look like you need it. Why don't you drive back to the hotel for a short nap? I'll come get you for dinner."

"It's been a long day," he said. "But I want to help out, Petey."

"You are helping. You helped all morning. You're helping right now."

Dwight let out a deep, wet sigh, and his eyes searched around the kitchen.

"You promise to call me for dinner, promise not to let me sleep all night and miss everyone?"

"You bet."

With as much calm as he could manage, Peter slid Dwight's keys across the island's countertop. But then Dwight's hand was on his shoulder.

"Do you know how proud my brother would have been to see you now—back from D.C., dressed up in your suit with your swanky lawyer job? He would have been so proud—was proud. He was so proud of you, your Daddy."

Peter's ears blushed. The compliments felt inverted, like they were stripping away pride rather than layering it.

"You know that if you ever need me ..."

"Come on, Dwight. Let's get some air."

"Here. Take this." He produced a card with the funeral director's name on it. On the back he had scrawled *Anytime!* with his various numbers—home, work, cell, and his e-mail address.

"Really, Pete. Your Daddy'd kill me if I didn't make sure that you was all right."

"Really. Thank you, Uncle Dwight." Peter took the card and laid it on the counter. "Come on now. Let's go take that nap."

Peter steered his uncle down the hallway and out to the garage. His wife, Aunt Ellen, was already at the hotel sleeping with her lifelong back injury, which appeared as soon as the first wave of food had been depleted.

Peter manipulated his uncle into the car and stood in the driveway quietly folding and unfolding the book of matches in his pocket. His uncle took forever simply getting the car started, but finally pulled away in a tight curve out of the cul-de-sac. But he didn't straighten the wheel out and slurred into the neighbor's freshly landscaped bed bordering the yard, its flat fieldstone rocks politely falling out of place. The car halted, the reverse lights flared briefly, and then mud shot out from under the tires, which only stopped after Peter ran over waving his arms.

Back inside to get the keys to the Lexus. The house was quiet except for distant sobbing. He hasn't kept track of all the guests. They're probably upstairs milling about his father's study, Peter thinks, going through his father's things, laying claim to items and memories. He wished he'd been able to inventory everything first.

His mom sat on her bed, her knees still a pedestal for the Bible, but her face now wrecked. He went to her and hugged her head to his chest. He was sure she'd been struck by grief, was now laboring under its dark cloud. She'd been crying long enough for her mascara to run down her cheeks—a tattoo of pain. There's nothing more frightening to see, Peter thinks. He was mumbling something conciliatory as she pointed to the half-cut-out paper clipping in her lap. "Read that tragedy," she said through sobs. It was his father's obituary. The words hit him like little pellets of data. He was mostly running his eyes over them in hopes of stopping her sobbing. He almost didn't catch the mistake. It was down near the end, in the "survived by" paragraph. "Edward Traxler is survived by his wife, Ellen, a homemaker, and their only son Peter; in addition to his younger brother Dwight Traxler and his wife Susan Hines Traxler, of Memphis.

"That goddamned reporter," his mother said. "Shit for brains."

"We'll get them to run a correction."

"It'll be too late. Nobody reads the corrections—especially for the obituaries." Here she was pummeled with fresh sobs.

"I have to take the Lexus," was all Peter could think to say. "I've got to drive Uncle Dwight to his hotel. He just drove his car into Mrs. Sanderson's new landscaping. I think he might be a little drunk."

"Of course he's drunk," she said. "He's been drunk since he was 12."

"I'll be back in like 10 minutes."

"No hurry. I'll just be here—in the shit," she said. "Trying to track down that goddamned reporter," her tears morphing into anger and then back again. "Give my regards to my drunkard husband," she said, no longer crying, her face a death mask of rage, the shielding putty of her make-up having hardened now against her.

"I'm sorry, Mama," Peter said, which only brought back the tears.

When he got to the garage, Uncle Dwight was in the passenger's seat smoking his godforsaken menthols, flicking ashes out the window onto the clean concrete floor. Marrying Dwight Traxler to his mother in print was probably the worst offense the obit writer could have done. Had he taken a piss on his father's fresh grave, Peter's mom would have been less upset.

The hotel was a motel, the kind where you parked in front of your room and had to walk upstairs.

Aunt Ellen was sitting propped up in the bed when they got there, her feet gauzed in hose. Dwight went straight to piss and seemed to walk more sober in front of Aunt Ellen. The room had that high cirrus haze of heavy smoking. Peter begged off requests from Ellen to stay a while, saying he had to get back, that he was needed, etc.

"Well, you'll call us before dinner, right?"

Then Peter explained about the car.

"You'll come get us for dinner, right?"

To which Peter answered yes, of course. He just had to run some errands and whatnot before then.

"Thank you for driving him home," she said. Then quietly, as if Dwight could hear over his flushing, "he's just so torn up about this. Loved that brother so. Cried damn near the whole way from Kentucky—and it was not his allergies, he assured me."

Dwight came out of the bathroom with a visible limp. "Well, my feet are just fucked," he said. His face was wet and red, either from tears or serious scrubbing.

"Well what's wrong, honey?"

"It's my goddamned feet again. Jesus. It's the goddamned toenails."

"He's been having terrible ingrowns lately."

"Goddamn," he said, moving to the chair next to the desk. "I think it's all the time in dress shoes."

"They started when he was working third shift at the Plaza Park," Ellen explained, "and I said it was because of all that walking, and I told him—*told* him—"

"Ah hell."

"—to tell his boss they needed an extra golf cart and do you know what? Do you know they wouldn't *get* an extra cart? Which was just one more reason not to keep suffering like that, but now even working the gate at the convention center, they *still* hurt."

Dwight grunted as he tried to double over to undo his shoelace.

"I think it's gotten worse," she said.

The laces were tightly knotted and his thick blunt fingers just flicked at them, and he sucked air heavily, and after a couple of minutes he gave up and pulled up all flushed, one vein pulsing across his forehead.

"I've gotta get these damn wingtips off."

"He can get the procedure done in an hour, but he's needed at work. He'd be on crutches. He couldn't walk. He'd probably need to be home six weeks."

"Six weeks?"

"Well, both feet, remember?"

Dwight bent over again and scratched at his laces, but then just rocked back with a sigh. As he came up, Peter met his gaze and knew he should leave right then. That if he wanted out, if he wanted to get back to Mother, who's surely wondering where the hell he is, he'd better leave now.

"Petey," he said, lifting his left foot and joggling it at him, the sole scuffed into a whole new color, "want to help an old man out?"

Peter wondered if his mother was still crying back home, wondered if some extended family would reemerge from the shadows to fetch her water, replenish her Kleenex, to take his place.

Peter knelt down before Dwight's feet. The shoes were creased, wrinkled, a taut broken skin. He began with the left. For all of Dwight's thick-fingered, thick-tongued physicality, his laces were tied tight—double-knotted, the laces pulled like a doctor's stitching. After a couple of minutes of clawing, Peter finally coaxed out the double knot, and so the rest of the untying was fairly easy.

Dwight sat back, stared at the TV, breathed through his mouth. His immense belly hovered above. Peter loosened the laces, pried awake the dead leather tongue and began to work the shoe off the foot. Once the shoe cleared the heel it slid off easily. The sock was navy with one gold-stitched line at the toe. It looked like some sort of animal—the blind kind that lived underground.

Then the smell hit, and Peter began working on the other shoe so as not to think about it. But the smell was right there in his face—thick, heavy, meaty, musty. Thick with the sweaty cooped up rot of old man's feet, a swamp of cotton and flesh, a bog of overturned peat. Peter kept at the other knot, hoping his disgust wasn't showing.

"The sock," Dwight said. Peter didn't understand. Dwight leaned over and rocked back, so Peter quit the right foot—he'd just broken the double knot—and peeled off the first foot's sock like a banana.

Dwight winced. "Damn, son. You didn't have to pull my hair off." He lifted his foot to inspect it, causing Peter to rock back out of the way onto his haunches.

"Well shit fire," Dwight said, looking at the foot. "Ellen, look at that."

"Well, I declare. Dwight honey, are you all right?"

"Yeah, but goddamn."

"I told you you needed to get that—"

"Aw hush it. Petey, I guess just put the sock back."

Peter had recoiled. The foot was bloody from the ankle down. Some of it had dried and smeared and clotted with the hair on the top of his foot. The source seemed to be in the toes. Dwight lowered his foot and Peter looked closer. The bed of the toenail on his big toe was the source.

The toenail itself was thickened with age, the surface craggy, grayish, continental plates buckling. It looked more like a thick plastic scab than a toenail. The blood deep in the creases between his toenail and toe was still fresh, shiny.

"The other foot, too?" Peter asked.

"Well, it hurts. Who knows what it looks like?"

Peter undid the remaining knot on his right foot, slid the shoe off and was confronted with the first foot's twin—more of the same smell, the same suppressed humid heat. Peter peeled the navy blue sock off. Dwight's shins had an older man's smoothness, a bone of hairless white running up its edge. There was blood here too on this foot, thought not nearly as much. There was a little on his big toe and a couple of the nearby smaller toes. Dwight lifted his foot to inspect it over the hill of his belly.

"Houston, we've got a problem."

"I *told* you."

They went into it, their combative routine. Peter usually only saw them at Christmas, down from Kentucky, and each year they were the same, a little fatter perhaps, grayer, but always bickering about everything, both trivial and not—the meaning of life or the location of someone's keys, what time should they head for home, how best to back out of the driveway, who'd called dibs on the remote.

With the bloody feet it was no different. They would pause to watch the golf game on TV in between jabs at one another, keeping the fire stoked until the next commercial break. Peter went for the ice bucket and warm water. He grabbed the morning's used towels, moldering in a pile behind the bathroom door. He soaked them in hot water in the tub. He made a little operating theater pallet before Dwight's feet. He thought of moving Dwight to the bathroom, but that would just have been too complicated. Besides, Dwight was now deeply into the golf game above Peter's head.

"Did you see that?"

Peter grabbed the bar of soap, the thin, insubstantial hotel kind. The good thing about blood was that it washed off fairly easily. Peter scrubbed the right foot, the less bloody one, first. It came clean except down near the wick of his toenail, but Peter moved to scrub the left foot before tackling any kind of crevices.

"Will you look at that? The man's a machine, a pure machine. Pure-fection."

"Did your mother want us to bring anything?" Ellen asked.

"It's all in the stance. His stance is perfect. Every time, the exact same. He's like a statue. Nothing bothers him. It's like there's not even a crowd there. See there—"

"I told the Tubbels that we'd make gumbo later and they got excited. I didn't tell your mom. With everything going on I figured the less she thought about what she ate, the better."

"See that—he tips his hat after he sinks his putt. That's it. Nothing else. And it's not like he's tipping his hat to the crowd even. It's like he's tipping his hat to God."

"That Mr. Tubbel was such a nice man. So talkative. I can't believe he and Edith—that her name?—I can't believe they broke up. How long has that been now?"

Peter worked steadily. It didn't seem like his responses were needed.

The towels were bruised with blood splotches and Dwight's feet gleamed, except still for the toes. Peter grabbed one of the Styrofoam cups stacked near the miniature coffee pot and dunked and poured water in a concentrated fashion over the big toe of his right foot and then his left. This, for the most part, worked. His feet now almost looked normal, except for the warped, ragged toenails and the bursting maps of varicose veins at his ankles.

"I'd always hoped your mother wouldn't become one of those divorcers like the rest of them. They just seem so bitter."

"Peroxide?" Peter asked.

"Yeah, there's some in my bags with my make-up. Do you want me to get it?" she asked without moving, but Peter was up already unzipping various bags. Inside her two large, wheeled traveling bags were multiple clear cubes of zipped plastic, which contained every kind of make-up product from the last 15 years, products Aunt Ellen had no doubt never worn: concealers, blushes, brushes, small little rake-like combs, mascaras, eyelash poofers, pressers, pencils for the eyes, eyebrows, the outer contour of the lips. It was like stumbling on the make-up kit in a theater's greenroom. Then in a baggie filled with a variety of exfoliating and acne prevention products, he saw a bottle of hydrogen peroxide, not in a travel-sized miniature but in a big, two-handed economy size. He returned to Dwight's feet which sat patiently, shining on the clean towel. He picked up the right foot and poured the peroxide over the big toe into the cracks between the nail and the surrounding flesh—the source of the wound. The crease fizzled moderately, and Peter sighed to himself. The old man's falling apart, he thought. He dried the foot and took up the left one and poured again. The frothing of the peroxide was much worse, the vigorous frothing of infection.

"Jesus, Dwight," he said.

"What?"

"You've got to get this checked out. Your ingrowns are all infected."

"Well how bad are they?"

"I don't know. I'm not a doctor. Just get them looked at."

"Well how bad could it be?"

"Jesus. Just go. You could lose your feet, okay? If you don't get this cleaned up, it'll spread and one day it'll be too late and you'll have to say goodbye to your goddamned feet."

"Who's losing their feet?" Ellen asked.

Peter gathered up his gear. These people were hopeless. Before long I'll have to help them go to the bathroom, he thought.

He piled the towels outside the bathroom, washed out his ice bucket, and scrubbed his hands, all the while refusing to look himself in the mirror. He was still dressed in his coat but had sweated through his undershirt. He was constantly sheathed in cold.

"Do you want to stay and watch the rest? Tiger's kicking ass."

"No, I'd better go check on the house."

"You'll come get us for dinner?"

"Sure, sure. I'll call. Sure."

Peter paused for a second, watching them both, waiting for some type of moment to transpire. But they were both transfixed by the TV, and they hollered at it at the same time, as if it could hear their cheers.

Back in the Lexus, sealed in quiet, he cranked the car and put his hands at 10 and 2 on the steering wheel. His shirt cuffs peeked out of his jacket's sleeves. His hands were clean but his cuffs were rimmed in Dwight's blood.

Back at the house, silence downstairs, laughter upstairs. A shrieking hoot—Aunt Agnes, his mother's sister. Her laugh was as distinct as a fingerprint and distinctly annoying, knowing no range of intensity or volume control. Lush.

They'd been in the kitchen. The counter had a collection of overturned beer caps and various casseroles had been broken open, the rib cages of their foil pried back for messy surgeries. Overhead the funeral had turned into a reunion with the insulated footsteps and the boomy indistinctness of different relatives' voices catching up. This must be what heaven is like, he thought, a party where no one has to do the dishes.

The door to his mother's bedroom was mostly closed. He went in quietly. She was asleep. She'd toppled over from her station with the obituary. The clipped paper and scissors and tape and Bible had all scattered from her body. Peter collected the artifacts, pulled up the bedspread, cut off the bedside lamp, shining like some detective's interrogation light. Aunt Agnes shrieked overhead.

His mother's hair was still red, "burnished" he used to think of it in college, when he'd first heard that word, cropped short, gently curled, the auburn color seeping into a darker blood orange density toward the roots.

He sat in the rocking chair across the room. The clock said 5:22. It was a Saturday. His extended family laughed and sighed above him. He sat forward in the rocker, his elbows on his knees, his fingers interlaced before him, his bloody cuffs out around his wrists. Overhead, a laugh came out so hard it sounded like a sneeze. His mother slept on. Peter, from his seat in the corner of the master bedroom, kept watch, waiting for his mother to wake, waiting to discuss what she'd like for dinner, waiting to see what he might be able to provide. Still, still, he sat perfectly still, on earth as it is in heaven.

The Portable Son

By the time Peter got back to D.C., all he wanted was sex with Wendy. Shuffling onto the plane that next morning, his mother terribly depressing in her not-crying, he sat in his window seat and stared out onto the white pavement, imagining flesh—his erection the happy thought that buoyed him along the 1,000 miles, the plane intermittently shaking like an invalid in the high winds. He was up in her studio, the brakes of the Dupont Circle buses shrieking below, her mattress pushed up against the window, the tall rectangle of clear moon-air shining down on them, swaddled in sheets, the rhythm of their fluctuating body temperature, first too hot, then too cool, and back again. It wasn't until the plane skipped across the surface of the runway that he remembered how his mother had discovered the body: sitting upright in his idling car, strapped in his seatbelt, still in the garage, his father all ready to go somewhere.

 C3

Back at work by noon, only a half day ahead of him. On his desk was an oversized card signed by everyone from his practice group. Blondie presented it to him first thing along with a nearly tearful face and a hug, for which Peter held on too long. The saddest part of the day was the fact that he couldn't tell everyone how happy he was to be back. He couldn't even tell Blondie he'd missed her.

Out of a mute sense of sympathy for his father's heart attack, Blondie refused to give him any work, so Peter spent his time erasing conciliatory voicemails and chatting with the occasional well-wishing visitor. He was terribly bored. He wanted the thrilling monotony of going over claim files with Blondie, her perfume indistinct but noticeable, like a spirit overhead, somewhere near the buzzing fluorescent lights.

He spent time studying his card. It had a springtime meadow on its glossy surface, all bursting buds and fresh-washed greenery. The printed message inside was so curled up within its own font that he didn't bother reading it. It was the handwritten notes that interested him. Blondie's was nothing special, a few sentences praising his performance at the Firm. It was written in the same voice she used in meetings with her superiors: her résumé voice. The other signatures were a parade of easy clichés, much more anonymous than their actual faces. (Even Frankie from Receiving had written!) Finally, he found Richard's, the one he had been looking for, scratched in a boxy, microscopic print.

Peter, So sorry about your loss. Welcome to it. It's getting through this shit that makes us stronger. Drink it up. Your friend, R.

Peter stilled, dry-mouthed, the card sliding in his moist fingertips. He reread the note. Once more. He tried imagining it in Richard's voice. He read it aloud, quietly (his door was open). He studied the sturdy print, the way the letters marched in all equal sizes one after another, words evenly spaced, no sign of hesitation as to what to say, how much space it will take up, reconsiderations of tone, implication, inflection. What could it mean? "Your friend?" How many times had they actually spoken? Once on the Ledge, twice at Friday happy hours, the occasional hall head-nod, and then there was that one time at the keg at Elizabeth Shacklebury's house-party. Your friend. Did he mean to say "you're a friend"?

The longer he stared, the more puzzled he became. At three Blondie arrived with a chest full of files, but said they were so not important and that they could wait until whenever he felt like it and that she hated even bringing them. The card cast a shadow over the corner of his desk. Even when he pulled it to himself and reread the message and even when he compared its tone, word choice, handwriting style to other, more generic messages, he couldn't fathom what it meant.

At four he stepped out onto the Ledge to smoke. The Ledge was what they called this out of the way balcony, which had once been a private space for a partner in the Firm. But due to various transgressions, some of which occurred on this balcony and all of which were not discussed openly, the lawyer was no longer with the Firm and his office had been turned into the 9th-floor break room.

Peter pulled out a book of matches he had stolen from the funeral home and the pack of cigarettes he'd discovered while getting dressed on the day. Much to his mother's annoyance, he had come home for his father's funeral without a coat. He had left his one good navy blazer in D.C. His mother asked how this could happen, but it was easy, actually. Coats weren't required of the paralegals, just a tie and an acquaintance with an iron. In fact, regularly wearing a coat would have been improper, Peter had thought. He wanted to be known around the office, but not as uppity.

So his mother had sent him upstairs to his father's closet and he had looked for something appropriately dark. He found a deep chocolate brown sports jacket, and though it hugged him too forcefully around the shoulders, he didn't feel like trying on another. Walking back to his room, he felt a small, rectangular weight over his left breast. It was a pack of cigarettes, just six left. There was no telling how old they were, though they still held their lazy smell. His father had officially quit two years ago, after a bad physical and pressure from the family. So Peter wasn't sure if these were from a past life or a more recent, secret one.

"That shit'll kill you, ya know," Richard said, stepping out onto the Ledge.

"Yeah. That's what I hear."

"Nobody gets breaks for gum anymore," he said, plucking a small plug of gum out of his mouth and placing it into the ashtray. "The good thing about smoking out here is you can flick your butts on people's heads."

Peter laughed, and they both leaned over the railing and stared at the street. Busy head tops going nowhere.

"I didn't know you smoked," Richard said.

"I don't, really," Peter said. "I just thought I'd give it a try."

"I get it."

"You want one?"

Richard cut his eyes to him and puckered his lips.

"Sure. Why not."

Peter delicately plucked a second cigarette from the pack, his fingers counting over and securing and checking the others. He'd smoked one after the funeral, late; there were just three left.

After a moment of silent smoking, Richard said, "So how'd the day go?"

"It's been okay. Everyone's been real nice. And I practically had to pry some work out of Blondie."

"Yeah, she's a piece of work. You get the card?"

"Yeah, thanks."

"Good. That was all Blondie. I meant what I said though."

"I read it. Thanks."

"This shit'll make you stronger."

"Yeah. I see what you're saying."

"When my father died," Richard began, peering over the railing and exhaling, like he was blowing the smoke on the people down there, "it was good for us, good for the family, I mean. It brought us together. My sisters and my mom, for instance. We all had to work some stuff out. When a father goes like that, everyone's looking for who'll be in charge. Who's gonna take his place. You got brothers and sisters?"

"No."

"Just you? Well, that's okay, too. I'm sure it'll bring your mom and you closer. And maybe like aunts and uncles and whatnot. It might even be better in this case. In my family there were four boys and two girls—Catholic, obviously. When he died, everyone was in there trying to be Pops."

"Do you want another cigarette?"

Peter was holding the stubbed out butt of his, but Richard was only halfway through.

"No, that's all right. You okay?"

"Oh yeah. I'm totally fine. Why?"

"No reason. You coming to happy hour this week?"

"I don't know. I hadn't thought about it. Maybe."

"You should."

"Yeah. I've been a few times."

"It's a good opportunity."

"To network, yeah I know."

"Aw fuck that. Come for the drinks. After two or so, Blondie gets all huggy."

ೞ

After getting off work, Peter went straight to Wendy's studio—ten minutes later than he'd wanted, but Richard had stopped by his office to recruit him for the Firm's softball team. One of his roommates had called earlier to say she'd stopped by and left a purple iris and a hand-painted postcard. He was aching for a reunion.

He had met Wendy last fall, and it wasn't long before the extracurricular drunken hook-ups that had been his main solace stopped altogether and he was hiking up the steps to her studio every day. She lived and painted there alone, using her sole battered mattress for the occasional model. She worked during the day in a bookstore and Peter had no idea how she afforded the place. Once, he had seen this swarthy guy leaving in the afternoon, older, slick in a pin-stripe suit. "Oh, that's just Andrew," she had said.

In early February, a week before he got the job at the Firm, Peter came down with a kidney stone. He was coming home from his interview, riding the escalator up from the pit of the Metro, and as he stepped off, he doubled over with what felt like a sharp knuckle twisting in his right lower back. He staggered to Wendy's and she took care of him all weekend, feeding him soup and Vicodin, letting him sleep on the mattress.

All weekend Wendy pleaded with him to go see a doctor, but he refused. At first, he just ignored her, but late Sunday, after an afternoon of badgering, he told her that he didn't have insurance. But she called his bluff and found his Blue Cross, Blue Shield card in his wallet. When she demanded an explanation, he said, "I don't have any insurance that's not my parents'." "Your insurance. Their insurance. It doesn't matter where it comes from. You've got it," she said. "Now go."

That was their first fight and Wendy's first declaration that Peter had serious issues with his parents, calling him Oedipally underdeveloped, dredging up the whole Christmas situation, asking if he'd ever even rebelled, broken any laws, done anything to disappoint them. Peter just lay back in his haze. By Monday night, everything was back to normal: the pain passed, Wendy calmer. He got the job that next week.

Peter had rehearsed his next trip home and in his mind it had gone quite differently. His father was still alive, and Peter had kept his promise to himself and not flown home again until he could pay for it all himself. Never again the "you've got to make your own way" talk he had undergone over Christmas, when he was seven months out of school and still sending out résumés. He had envisioned taking the late afternoon flight home from Dulles, with the requisite layover in Atlanta, emerging in the terminal still in his shirt sleeves, his leather shoulder bag swinging at his hip, his look tired, sweaty, triumphant. He imagined his father asking how his day was, asking if he missed anything important by cutting out early, asking what Peter might have to do to make it up, and then Peter's practiced, nonchalant answer, "Nothing I can't handle," and his father's knowing, male laugh.

Wendy hugged him briefly, but was all business cleaning up, putting paints away, kicking the mattress into the corner. Peter trailed behind her, hugging her shoulders when she paused. She would kiss him quickly and squeeze his hand and keep moving. He wanted the kisses to last longer, the hugs to increase in pressure. When she told him it was time to go to dinner, he dallied and then began to pout as she dragged him down the stairs.

At dinner, Peter ate up the time in beer.

Afterward, Wendy wanted to show him something. So they began walking down the Mall. Peter perceived this gesture in multiple sexual ways, though he tried to keep his interpretations silent. Soon they were at the Lincoln Memorial and Peter's head was filled with thoughts of public sex. They walked up the great marble steps, Wendy's haunch above his head, baiting him on. When she reached the landing, she stopped to rest, and Peter enveloped her in his arms, in his breath, kissing near her ear, looking over the side of her head up to the crotch of the great, seated forefather.

"Seriously, Pete. Lay off," she said, pinching her shoulders and scuttling away like a bird. She kept moving up the steps, didn't even turn around and kiss him softly, offering some type of mute, physically expressed rain check, only kept always out of reach. Peter marched sullenly after her.

She led him behind the monument where through the columns shone a highway and then further, the Potomac. She walked him to the center and sat down on the edge, her feet dangling off the side. Peter stood above her.

"This is it," she said. "Sit down."

Before he could respond, she said, "Isn't it nice?"

The moon had risen and shone over the Potomac, which was caught in mid-bend, the curve of the water mimicking the highway. Wendy sat on her hands, her feet slightly kicking.

Peter, gradually accepting the idea that she was not about to manipulate parts of his body, sighed and sat down.

They sat for a few minutes, not talking but listening to the cars whispering by below.

"Don't you like it?" she said. "This is my favorite spot in the whole city, much better than being out front with the tourists. I usually only come here by myself."

"It's nice," Peter said. He couldn't think of anything else to say. She was at least now burrowed beside him, holding his hands as he steadily rubbed bits of dried paint off her fingers. He'd always loved Wendy's hands, the way they looked grade-school small and wind-bitten, the way she never painted her nails, almost in contrast to the paint that was always crusting over her small fingers. The paint peeled and flaked and curled into tiny dried wrinkles, revealing the soft pink underneath as Peter rubbed.

"So will you tell me about him?" she asked, finally breaking her stare at the river.

"What do you want to know?"

"Anything," she said. "Something you'll always remember."

Sitting behind the monument, the moon shining on the water and the passing cars, his mind hummed vacantly, swerving between intimations of sex and the aged pack of cigarettes still in his shirt pocket. The wind whipped around them. It was now dark and cool in the shadow of the monument, and they huddled together on the edge, Peter busily, silently cleaning her hands and trying to remember something.

ᘓ

Early summer. Blondie was burying him in work and lingering in his office at approximately 4:15 every day. Her leather couch, ordered from Italy, had arrived, and Blondie joked how her husband had Jewed the guy down on the price. ("You *hafta* come try it out," she kept telling him.) Peter had become a regular at Friday Happy Hour, where he leaned against the bar alongside Richard and surveyed the crowd. The softball team, now 3-1, was finding its rhythm.

He talked to his mother every other day. In mid-March, when he'd first gotten back, he called her, at a minimum, every night around 7:30 Central, just as she was finishing her supper. How was she? Tired. Any visitors? Gloria had dragged her out to lunch again. Any work opportunities? Helped stuff envelopes at the school. That Debbie Hazzard is a bitter old thing. And then, after the questions had been exhausted, the aria of grief would begin, exhumed from the casket of some terribly familiar family anecdote. Remember the time when you two were going to build treehouses for every kid in the neighborhood? And though he certainly remembered, she would replay the story, the tears building up and spilling as she reached that particular anecdote's unbearably moving ending. She would sob quietly on the phone for a couple of minutes and that would be all. Peter was then free to go find Wendy.

But now, by June, she was better, she was better, she was so much better. So good, in fact, that she'd begun to worry about him, and to find out for certain, she sent Lloyd. He had to come up for work, he'd said on the phone. But it was obvious to everyone that his mission's covert objective was to check in on Peter, paternally speaking.

They met on the river at a restaurant that served blue margaritas. It was a 15-minute, confusing, downhill walk from his apartment in Georgetown. They sat outside, the sun so bright their eyes watered. The wind jumped over the river and shook the skin of their table's blue umbrella. Yachts, freed from their winter hibernation, plowed down the Potomac beside them.

It actually felt good to see Lloyd. He brought news of Peter's mother—how she looked, how she was eating, how she was spending the money—in general, how she was assimilating to the concept of widowhood. (For starters, it did wonders for her social life. No longer cooped up in the house, knitting away on her stash of bitterness, she was now out, with people, doing things—middle-aged widow things—and was apparently exceedingly happy.) But since Lloyd was his mother's platonic friend and not, strictly speaking, kin, he could be politely blunt with Peter where his mother often became distracted, her sentences dwindling into mutters when confronted with a question she disliked.

And Lloyd looked good. His tall pink forehead shone in the sunlight, its blush bleeding into his fine, strawberry-blond hair. He had the overall look of being lacquered. And Peter could tell that he was happy to see him, the tanned hand slapping his shoulder as he steered him through the restaurant onto the veranda.

They had drinks with raw oysters while they waited on Wendy, Lloyd with a delicate flute of champagne and Peter sucking down a beer. Peter both did and did not want her there with them. But Lloyd had been so occupied with telling Peter about his mother that he hadn't yet interrogated him about his love life. When she finally got there, Peter had switched drinks and was halfway through his first margarita, which was neon blue and cold as a glacier, and being an amateur drinker (another subject he never mastered in college) he rose and tried to play the appropriate gentleman.

Part of this desire was brought out by Lloyd, who was always seen as the contemporary example of southern gentlemanliness. Even his father had thought so: "That dandy of your Mom's is closer to Robert E. Lee than anybody I ever met."

Then, the confusion of politeness. More drinks arrived. Everyone sat. Two minutes later Wendy and Lloyd were the best of friends. He asked her about her art and all Peter had to do was smile and nod. It was for the best. He could hardly begin his third margarita and his burger became difficult to chew, his head bobbing like a river buoy.

But after a quick salad, Wendy had to go. Remember, she had a meeting with the photographer? He did not remember. He felt dizzy with confusion and jealousy. They were all getting along so well. She didn't leave until she had traded e-mail addresses and phone numbers with Lloyd, who was simply positive he could arrange a meeting between her and a gallery owner in Atlanta and who simply demanded she send him some slides. They said goodbye with a cheek kiss and a hug.

Peter walked her back through the restaurant. The chilled air straightened him up inside slightly. "I don't recall ..." he began.

"Oh, relax, Petey. It's for the show in August."

Okay, that did sound slightly familiar. She kissed him with her open salty mouth as waiters circled. Peter could feel the hostess leer.

"I like your uncle," she said.

"He's not my uncle. He's just a friend of my mom's."

"Well, whatever he is, he's a doll," she said.

"Take me home with you," he said.

She patted him on the head. "Maybe another time, cowboy."

She smiled her beautiful, completely indecipherable smile and left, and as Peter walked back through the restaurant to his outside table, he was walking back to her apartment in his mind, his erection guiding him like a compass.

"That girl's to *die* for," Lloyd shrieked when Peter sat back down. "I mean, I know I'm not exactly the best person to give *you* relationship advice, and Lord knows I'm not the marrying kind, but if I were you ..."

"Oh, Lloyd, please. Don't go there."

"Go where? I'm just saying. She's just so ... so ... smart and charming and ... and beautiful ... and she obviously adores you and ..."

"Okay. Okay. I get your point."

"I mean, if I were, you know, in your shoes, well first, I wouldn't wear lace-ups, but secondly ..."

Peter kept his mouth shut. Lloyd's boiled red face glistened before him, clanging some foreign message. The meal had gone on too long. The afternoon had peaked. He was tired of sitting in his own sweat.

When they left the restaurant, they walked up the long hill back into Georgetown University itself. Lloyd was staying at the hotel on campus and wanted Peter to "walk the lunch off" with him.

It wasn't easy. Lloyd, despite the sophistication of his shoes, wasn't exactly sure which street he'd come down (he'd taken a cab), and Peter's mental fuzziness didn't help. All they knew was that they had to walk uphill. Peter began to sweat through his dress shirt, and each footstep fell in sync with the churning of his head.

"Should we cross over to O Street?" Lloyd said. Peter managed to shrug. His mouth felt like paper.

They turned right for a block, sliding sideways, turned back uphill for another block and repeated the process, zig-zagging like a winded kid trying to bike uphill.

Lloyd talked the whole way. "I mean really Pete, that girl is divine. Got a head on her like you wouldn't believe. And funny? I thought I was gonna shoot champagne through my nose. Your Mama'd be so proud. Not that I'm going to tell her a thing because that's none of her business. Not that it's anybody's business. But I tell you: you've done mighty fine for yourself here. Do you know that? Can you see that? Can you see how good you've done in—Hell, has it been even a year yet? Do you see what you've done? I'm so proud. I'm just so ... and do you know who else is proud—who else would be proud? Do you?"

"I think we're lost," Peter said, his dress shirt stuck to him like he'd just come out of the bath.

"Do you know?"

They turned left (back uphill) and there, miraculously, stood the gates of Georgetown.

"Perfect. Brilliant," Lloyd said.

Peter kept them moving uphill, filling the void with an abbreviated rendition of how cool and promising his job was.

And he did acknowledge Lloyd's approval, somewhere using the word "swell." And he did say, "I'm glad everyone's so proud back home," hoping to include in his vagueness both the living and the dead.

They stood inside the gate next to a flowerbed fenced off in miniature wrought iron spikes.

"Thanks for meeting me like this," Lloyd said.

"Sure. Yeah. You know, anytime."

"I really appreciate it. I think you and your Mama both are going to be a-okay."

"Thanks, man. I really, you know, appreciate you keeping an eye on her."

Lloyd nodded and with one hand he patted his hot pink face with a white handkerchief. His monogrammed initials winked between his fingers. In mid-pat, Lloyd's other hand was at Peter's chest, holding a crisp fresh green hundred-dollar bill folded into quarters.

"Put this somewhere safe," he said.

Peter clutched the money and only as his fingers touched the sharply creased edges did he realize what was going on.

"I can't do that, Lloyd," he said.

"Peter. I insist. Please."

"No, really. I'm fine. Really, Lloyd. I'm fine."

"I know you're fine. I'm not saying that. I'm just ... let it be a treat. Take that Wendy out for a nice meal somewhere. It's no big..."

"I'm fine. I've got a fine job."

"Come on, Pete. It's not that big a deal."

"I don't need your money, Lloyd. Okay?"

Lloyd kept his hand outstretched, the money just above Peter's breast pocket, the bill pinched between his knuckles. His face had dried and hardened and now looked older.

After a moment longer, he said, "All right. Suit yourself. No hard feelings, right?"

"No. Not at all. It's just ..."

"Hey, don't worry about it. You've got your reasons."

They embraced and Lloyd repeatedly patted his damp back and mumbled something low and warm and conciliatory, but Peter did his best not to hear, in fact did his best not to be comforted at all despite the comforting elements he couldn't completely ignore. After holding on too long, Lloyd parted, rubbing what might have been tears out of the wicks of his eyes with his handkerchief. He then glided off into the tree moss, hanging from the branches like rotted lace.

CB

Without thinking about it, and without even considering why he wasn't thinking about it, Peter stopped calling Wendy shortly after Lloyd's visit. When his mother asked about her by name a week or so later, he wasn't entirely lying when he said he hadn't seen her since that lunch on the river.

Wendy kept calling him for a week, but then must have taken the hint. He kept away from Dupont Circle, as much as his bus and subway commute would allow. He varied his routes home from the grocery store. He even walked four blocks in the opposite direction each morning to meet a new Georgetown bus. He was quickly pacing out a new life. But then, about four weeks later, she found him at a bookstore up on Wisconsin. Peter had hardly finished thumbing through a magazine when she appeared at his shoulder. "What's your damage, problem child?"

"What?"

"You're not gonna even call? Not going to say anything, just gonna fly off?"

Peter put back his magazine. Her cheeks were flushed, her skin red down to her clavicle. She held a sharpened pencil in her tiny right hand, gripped like a dagger.

"I guess so," he said.

"Well that pretty much fucking sucks, Peter."

"Lots of things suck, Wendy." He tried to say it hard, crisp, seal it with meaning.

She was shaking slightly, her lips parted, breathing through her mouth. She had her hair pulled back tight against her head and looked feral. Afterward, when he was more calm, Peter would debate with himself if she had been about to cry. She was less than a foot away. He could smell the coffee tinge to her breath.

"Wendy, listen. I didn't mean to ..."

"We were just leaving," she said, louder, and she spun around and was joined—he appeared from out of the bookshelves—by a companion, older, turtle-necked, swarthy, the man he had seen at her loft so long ago, Andrew. He was folding out a tip onto their café table, her purse pinched to his side with his elbow. He took her under his free arm and without paying Peter even a glance, they disappeared out the door into the rain. Their table had the trash of some date, a dessert plate smeared with icing and their two deflated cappuccinos, the inner rims of the mugs showing the high tide of the foam, and, on Wendy's, the half-moon of her lipstick.

ॐ

Not a week later, during one of her late afternoon assignment-visits, Blondie was leaning over Peter's desk beside him, chewing over data, their heads nearly touching. They were cowering over a spreadsheet of call signs, provisionally discussing their significance, but actually imitating their boss holding a meeting. Blondie's yellow blouse gaped in between buttons as she bent over. Her chalk-white bra glowed. And it was just after they had both finished giggling about something tremendously funny when Peter slipped his left hand in between the two securing buttons and ever so gently cupped her right breast, his thumb resting on her insulated nipple, just long enough for its coordinates to radiate through his body. In the next moment of consciousness, Blondie was standing in the doorway, at profile, her arms tightly knotted. There seemed to be no memory of Peter's hand coming out of her shirt, of her pulling away, walking away. That portion of the tape had been deleted. There was only Blondie standing sideways, saying, "That was totally not kosher, Traxler."

ଓ

"Want a cigarette?" asked Peter, already suited up in his spikes and the too-tight pin-stripe baseball pants, the ones he wore in eighth grade and never returned. It was mid-summer. The softball season was wrapping up, just in time for the absurd heat.

Richard glanced over his shoulder while lacing up his spikes, his forehead already sweaty.

"Not right now, chief. Maybe later," he said.

The season always ended just in time for everyone's elaborate Fourth of July plans. The question echoed through the office: *What're your plans for the Fourth?* Peter had none.

Working with Blondie was now strictly functional. No more giggling. She referred to him only as Traxler and always spoke in her résumé/meeting voice.

He hadn't seen much of Richard lately either. He was always on the phone or in some meeting, and at the softball games he played catcher and took things seriously, conferring with Blondie over his stats before most games, seeing how he was doing, how the team was doing. Peter had been holding up their end of the bar at Friday happy hours, always scanning the crowd.

Peter scratched into the row of bleachers just behind Richard.

"I don't think anyone would mind," Peter said. "It's not exactly like we're breaking a sweat."

Richard finished lacing his left cleat and plucked the other from the wad of gear, all of it caked in the orangey red dirt of the infield. He thwacked the cleat on the concrete twice, knocking off most of the dirt. "So how's work coming along, junior?"

Peter was staring at Richard's jersey which had the name *Barron* in sewn-on block letters. Underneath was the number 18. He had been meaning to ask Richard what he was doing for the Fourth. Peter was always forgetting things he'd saved up to ask him.

"It's fine," Peter said.

"Right."

"No problems."

"Right."

Richard began lacing up his other cleat.

"How are things working out with Blondie?" Richard asked.

A rod of self-consciousness shot through Peter. He tried not to move on the aluminum bleachers, but even his breathing seemed to reverberate.

"Oh fine. I mean, you know, she's great. I really think I'm learning a lot."

"Right. Yeah, she's good. She'll teach you all kinds of shit. You stick around long enough, there's no telling what you'll learn." He was looking up from his spikes, which scratched on the concrete.

"Yeah, I'm sure," Peter said, though he wasn't sure what he was agreeing with.

"How's that girl you been seeing? Wendy, that her name? You haven't said anything about her lately."

"Yeah, we haven't really been talking."

"Yeah? That's too bad." He was strapping his left shin guard to his leg. "Probably saved you from getting married though. I tell ya, if you hit six months and you're not in for the long haul, you'd best head for the hills. You may not be thinking about it, but I guarantee she is."

"Yeah."

"You bummed about it?"

"I'm not really bummed. I'm fine. I don't know. I hadn't really thought about it. Wendy, I guess."

Richard finished with the left shin guard, stood and adjusted it, and sat back down and began on the right leg.

"Richard, what are you doing for the Fourth?"

"What do you think I'm doing? I'm going to Baltimore to see my wife's family. We get anything longer than the standard weekend, and we're in Baltimore. That or they come here. I'll probably be buried in Baltimore. I don't know what it feels like to have a vacation anymore. It's ridiculous. But my wife—have you met my wife?"

Peter shook his head.

"I'll trot her out here sometime. Lovely lady. Anyway, what are you doing? You going to call that Wendy chick or what?"

"I don't know. I'll probably hang with my roommates, I guess. Got any suggestions?"

"Beats me. Go see the fireworks. Go get laid. Have you seen the fireworks?"

"I went and saw them last year."

"Oh, well then, I'm all out of suggestions. Maybe give that Wendy chick a call. Or somebody."

Peter watched Richard finish with the right shin guard and stand. He began to put on the chest protector.

"Do you have kids?" Peter asked.

"God no."

"Do you want to have kids?"

"What are you, my father-in-law? Here, strap me in."

Peter stepped over the bleachers to stretch the straps taut across the scratchy jersey. Richard was one of the only players who wore a real jersey on top, instead of just a T-shirt with the company's logo. Peter hooked the straps tight, making an X across his back.

"Are you Barron?"

"What's left of him."

"Can I go with you to Baltimore?" Peter said.

"What? You're kidding, right?"

Peter scraped backwards in his spikes, bumping into the clangy bleachers and holding himself from falling. Richard turned around, his chest now guarded in the horizontal bands of orange foam. He looked directly at Peter.

"Peter, you need to stay here with your friends and get laid," he said.

He picked up his hat and adjusted it backwards.

"What's with all this depression shit lately?" Richard asked.

"I'm fine," Peter said, sitting back down.

"Look," he said, "is it about this Wendy girl?"

"I'm fine, really."

"I mean, you've been all drag-assing around the office lately. Are you worried about the Blondie stuff?"

Peter was staring into the field, watching Heller, one of the partners, hit grounders to the in-fielders. There was only the metal ping of the bat followed by some clichéd coach's phrase: *good hustle, soft hands, keep your eye on it.*

"Don't worry about Blondie," Richard was saying over his head. "That shit'll pass over. She'll get over it. And you're not in trouble."

"I don't know what you're talking about," Peter said, his voice husky, scratchy like his spikes on the concrete.

"You're not going to be fired or anything. Hell, you just did what everyone's always wanted to do. You just gave her what she's always been asking for."

"I don't understand," Peter said.

"You can't let this shit drag you down, okay? Okay, chief? Am I making sense?"

"Sort of. I guess," Peter said.

Peter was trying to hold the tears in. His eyes were welling, and he knew if he blinked too violently, they would tumble down his face and he would lose another friend.

"Doesn't it, you know, get any better?" Peter said with a fake half-laugh, still watching the infield.

Richard positioned his hat and reached for his facemask. He looked out over the field where Heller kept pinging and shouting. Good hustle, Maddox. Good hustle, Johnston. Thataboy, Carlisle.

"Peter, when's the last time you talked to your mother?"

"Last night," Peter said, now looking down at Richard's legs, the shin guards streaked in scars, as if they'd been drug over pavement.

"That's good. How often you call?"

"Every other night."

"That's good. That's good," he said. "Here's the deal, Peter, about your problems you've been having. The only thing you have to worry about is calling your mother. Got me? Just keep that up. Everything else here is just optional."

He was gesturing with the face mask as Peter stared into the empty aluminum bench.

"Now, she still crying every time y'all talk?" he said.

"Yes."

"What do you tell her?" he said. "You tell her everything's going to be all right?"

"Yes."

"Say it even though you don't believe it, right? Keep telling her over and over?"

"Yes."

"Good. Now listen, my boy. All you've gotta do right now is convince your Mama that it's okay your Daddy died, got me? Everything else is gravy. Whose pussy you're gonna get and whose pussy you're not going to get—all that shit will work itself out. It's just like Heller says out there: soft hands."

He pulled the catcher's mask down over his face.

"Make sense, chief?"

"Yes sir."

"Good. Thus endeth the lesson. That's the only one I do, so don't come looking for any more wisdom," he said, chucking Peter on the shoulder with his mitt. "Now, time to go act young. Have a good goddamned game."

He clicked away to the opening in the fence behind the dugout. Heller whooped in greeting, asked where the hell he'd been.

Peter sat back down on the bleachers as the aluminum bat continued to tap out its message to the infield. The spot on the bleachers was still warm from Richard's sitting. The momentum in Peter's abdomen had peaked and diminished like a bike coasting downhill and he could feel his heart pulsing, seemingly heavier now, seemingly turned back on. Otherwise, he felt empty and sat with his back straight, his hands resting on the caps of his knees, his own cleats now quiet on the concrete.

The sun in its afternoon light was behind his head and cast its shadow across his shoulder. He looked to the infield, saw Richard warming up the pitcher, squatting behind the plate, his mouth an engine of gab. *Thatababy lemme have it snotfire.* He became a completely different man when he went on the field. In the office, he was detached and wry and cool, but out here he was always dirty, always talking. Everyone loved him.

He saw Blondie approach from the parking lot with her statistician's notebook clutched to her chest and a purse bouncing against her hip. Peter wondered if Wendy would show up, flying in on some happy thought mid-game and sitting at the top of the bleachers, sketching. It could happen. She had done it once, sometime before the lunch with the blue margaritas.

He pulled out the sat-on pack of cigarettes from the back pocket of his jersey pants. Two left, bent but not yet broken. A mini Bic lighter rattled around inside with them, and their smell arose gently from the bent foil.

He should leave right then, he thought. He and the cigarettes should find her. But the game was about to start. It was time for him to move to the dugout.

The weight of the sun bore down on Peter's shoulders, pressing his body onto the bleachers. The nearly empty pack of cigarettes was all he could hold. He felt so much like a failure but had no one to fail for anymore.

Popular Baggage

His name was Jason Stiph and he was the hardest working kid in school. He was never the smartest kid, only the one who had apprehended his family's near-failure. His father had done something vaguely horrible when Stiph was a boy. I could never find out what. He'd spent several years in prison, but was back with the family and repentant. Consequently, Stiph had developed this hyperventilating will to succeed: like at the science fair, where he got second place for testing the viscosity of various types of synthetic oil, using a disembodied engine block he'd rigged with one of his south Jackson neighbors; and at sports, when he tried out for football sophomore year even though he had never played, wasn't an ounce over 160, and was later disinvited from the team for his own safety; and in social circles, Stiph was no less a boy who yearned to achieve, who refused to believe in social circles because he wanted to penetrate them all. Exhibit A: Sarah Samson.

The problem began back in late February of '96 during senior year. He was prancing down the hall toward me looking like he had just made the starting five in basketball. He had just asked—he announced between victorious sips from a fresh Dr. Pepper—Sarah Samson to prom. She had accepted.

Never mind that Sarah Samson was absurdly popular, probably one of the top five most desirable and therefore most avoidable females at Niskayuna. Never mind that prom was still seven weeks away and that the only people who got dates this early were desperately overeager. Never mind that SS was a prom date of, shall we say, significant complications. And yet, despite all of this, he was ebullient, overjoyed, shining from the heat of his own courage. And yet somehow, as a friend, I had to speak truth to this predicament. Wouldn't you?

"This endeavor is going to be seriously complicated," I said.

"Complicated how?" he asked.

"Well, maybe complicated isn't the right word. It's just ... taking SS? She's awfully popular."

"So?"

"Well, that's complicated," I said. "It gets complicated. It can get complicated."

"Complicated."

"Well, she's *really* popular, and she's got a lot of baggage tied up in an event like this."

"What kind of baggage?"

"I don't know. Popular baggage."

"Right."

Sarah Samson was captain of the cheerleading squad, the one cheerleader who could actually tumble and do other gymnastic-like things. She wore this authority lightly, constantly chipper and bubbly and faux-ditzy. It was all very grating. When she appeared from beneath that mask at times of great stress—say, the previous fall's homecoming pep rally when half of "her" squad was too drunk to cheer straight—her true nature was revealed, and it was thrifty, cold, and severe.

We were sort of acquaintances since I was the DJ for the pep rallies and she cut the checks. So we had long heart-to-hearts whenever the squad wanted to renegotiate my fee, which I never lowered. She was a brunette with pale porcelain skin, which could, as Stiph had mentioned more than once, blush in the most fantastic way. It began at the base of her neck, would flood up her cheeks, and the color would just sort of hang there and pulse. She also had, it must be said, two of the most exquisite calves I've ever seen. They were gigantic, flashing with wonderful muscle definition at certain points during a routine. They were the kind of calves that you simply couldn't work on; they were the kind you were born with. Once, when I was at her house, I tried to spy on her mother's legs to see if it came from her, but the woman was covered up in mom jeans so who knows.

Stiph, everyone knew, was in a different league. His love life reminded me of certain families, the ones that seem to attract disaster—a child's spinal injury here, a father's accidental death there—so that after the first couple of seemingly freak but all-too-coincidental tragedies strike, everyone wants to pull stakes and avoid contamination. Though I hadn't been friends with Stiph that long—we weren't like friends for life or anything—I had discovered that he was chronically obtuse with local girls but always managed to have these vague long-distance relationships which usually climaxed (and then quickly ended) with a trip to Jackson. So the best I could say about SS was that at least she was local. His prom record, however, was the worst part about him. The year before, he'd asked this girl from like Alabama or something—again extremely early—and she didn't even show up.

Her name was Amy and he had met her through regional choir competitions the previous fall. They had hit it off and had been talking back and forth over the phone for months. He asked her to prom in like November. No wonder she changed her mind.

I didn't see her until the next fall. Over the summer, Stiph had convinced me to join choir for my senior year even though I couldn't sing. (He said it would be good for my college apps since

DJ-ing didn't really qualify as a viable extracurricular.) I usually just stood up there and mouthed along. Well, when we went to regionals again the next year, she was there with her school, some elite little mountain-top school in Birmingham.

The whole shebang was in Memphis at this dingy Holiday Inn. We saw her in the first group rehearsals, and I almost fell off the risers. She was tall with pale skin and board-straight red hair. (Stiph wasn't what you would call handsome: his thick, generic, blond-brown hair never really could be combed, only wetted and directed. His torso was too long for his legs so that he looked put together from scrap parts. He had large, frequent freckles, lightly fuzzy.) Both Ronald and I—Ronald was Stiph's other friend who was around even before me—were shocked at her beauty but we didn't make a big deal about it. We still carried out our plans of revenge. We borrowed three ties from her classmates at her elite school. They all wore uniforms with maroon ties. We waited for her to walk back to the elevators after her rehearsal and we all stood in front of the doors, blocking her way, with the maroon ties dangling out of our zippers. And of course giving her the finger. Not talking or even heckling her. Just standing in her way, making our presence known.

She had avoided us completely the next day, somehow blending in despite that glowing tower of hair. We put phase two of the revenge plan into effect. I skipped rehearsal and set up the doll in the lobby and uncovered her just before everyone came back to the hotel for dinner. One of the hotel clerks was giving me a look the whole time but I knew he didn't have the balls to actually say anything. When people started pouring in to the foyer next to the elevators, they saw our creation: a blow-up doll, her plastic mouth molded into a circle, her top half covered in a cheerleading jersey from her school. I had sat her on one of those ashtray-trash can combos. The poster above her said:

Hi. My name is Amy. I'll huff and I'll puff and I'll blow your house down.

And then thinking that was too confusing, I scratched through the last bit and wrote, *and I'll blow this whole hotel.*

People began to congregate. We didn't see her anymore after that. Later, after we got back to Jackson, I heard that her mother had driven up from Birmingham that night to take her home.

☙

"It's just she's going to have to visit with lots of people," I kept telling him in scattered conversations over the next few days. "That's how they are: there's going to be a lot of forced socializing, hitting all the right bases, hugging all the right necks. They're worse than politicians, these girls."

"And so—what? You don't think I should go with her?" he said.

"No, that's not what I said at all. It's just—it's just a matter of personal attention."

"I should give her more personal attention?"

"No. That's not it. It's just the *quality* of her attention is not going to be what you think it's going to be."

"She's not stupid, Peter. What is your beef against her?"

"That's not what I'm saying at all."

These conversations went on forever, it seemed. I couldn't figure out a way to get my point across without either A) crushing his spirit or B) him smacking me over the head. He seemed very defensive about the integrity of this "date," even its definition as a full-fledged "date." I finally gave up after going with him to rent his tuxedo.

"Can you get a refund on that thing?" I asked the clerk. Stiph had not been able to get a refund the year before. It was now a full four weeks before the big day, and we were at the mall. Stiph had already added gloves and a top hat to his order.

"What do you mean?" the clerk asked.

"I mean, like if we need to can we return the tux and get a refund?"

"Why would you be able to get a refund?" the clerk asked. He seemed amazed at my question, like a scholar with a young student.

"Like if you don't wear it. Like if the party's going to fall through?"

"If the party has fallen through, why would you pick up the tuxedo?" the clerk said.

Stiph didn't even say anything, didn't have to. He just stared me down and pushed over his fat fold of dirty money. So from then on I just shut my mouth and let him ride.

ങ

But I wasn't as deluded as Stiph thought. I heard it just the very next week—their plans for a coup. It happens every year. Some girl doesn't want to go with some poor guy—it's always some *girl*—and so she ditches him at some party. And my paranoia regarding SS wasn't exactly unfounded. She didn't have the best reputation as a reliable date. There was Morris Dickey, whom she'd abandoned halfway through the Homecoming dance our freshman year. There was Tommy Wallace, with whom she'd gotten into a screaming match at Florence Devereux's party that next spring. And then, of course, there was the mysterious Brad, whom she had dated intensely the entire fall before and who had made only one appearance at a Niskayuna-related function and who—rumor had it—actually had only one testicle. Didn't Stiph remember any of this?

I was setting up my DJ stuff at the Friday pep rally. We had pep rallies damn near year-round at Niskayuna; the administration thought it good for morale. I was stacking the mains and hooking up the speaker cables and getting everything ready for liftoff when I overheard SS talking with her fellow comrades. I did the DJ-ing not so much for the money but for this oasis of freedom: the 90 minutes I had convinced the administration to allow me to set up and break down the gear. It was that blissful time when everyone was still in class except us. The girls were all stretching on the floor with their legs spread, swiveling around on their hips, their bare skin squeaking on the lacquer. Maybe the Niskayuna administration was onto something. I'd always found the site of those innocent unadult legs heartening, especially in winter, barely covered in those navy blue pleated skirts.

"Who exactly came up with 'A Night on the Nile'?" one of them asked.

"I like it."

"It's so lame."

"What exactly is it? I mean, what *is* 'A Night on the Nile'?"

"It's the Nile. You know, like Egypt and the pharaohs and stuff."

"Is this like a costume party?"

"No, no."

"Well you know who's already got a date."

"Oh yeah."

"Shut up, y'all."

"Did he get down on one knee?"

"Doesn't he seem ... maybe a little excited?"

"Shut up."

"He's sweet."

"Well yeah he's sweet. My little brother is sweet."

"*Y'all.*"

"She'll have fun."

"Oh yeah."

"Why don't you just say no?" asked the freshman, an alternate who had gotten on the team after Kristjen Holsey broke her ankle.

"She can't just say no."

"Well why not?" asked the freshman.

"You don't want to be *mean.*"

"But if she ..." said the freshman.

"Are you excited?"

"Gosh, y'all, I don't know. Not really. But I mean, I couldn't *not* say yes. He was so—"

"I told you: he's been smiling like crazy in calculus."

"He always looks like that in calculus."

"It doesn't matter, anyway. You don't have to stay with him the whole night."

"Is Robert going to have his party?"

"Oh yeah."

"How could she do that?" asked the freshman.

"Easy. Get sick. Get Cramps. Tell him the food makes you nauseous."

"Really?" asked the freshman.

"Oh, yeah. Nobody actually leaves with the same guy. Not if they don't want to."

They giggled and moved on to other subjects. I was trying not to listen, or just trying not to appear like I was listening. I slid my headphones on. I kept my eyes on the board, the knobs, the channel buttons, the volume slides. I was twisting, tweaking, turning, adjusting the sound to fit my ear though there wasn't any music playing.

CB

The year before, when Stiph got ditched by that Amy girl, I was still with Melissa Wells. She was, as they say, the one. The spring of '95 was the peak of our relationship. It was fouled by summer break, among other things, but we had continued to hang out together in an undefined way for most of the next school year. And when Stiph dropped me off after our little trip to the tux store, I decided I should go to prom that year, too. I wasn't planning on it originally. Though Melissa and I were still technically speaking, it was still destined to be forced. And I sure didn't think I'd be able to get her alone in a car anytime soon.

In that spring of '96, Melissa had just begun to forgive me for Valentine's Day. I had, regrettably, rigged the school's week-long secret admirer gift-giving game so that she was my target/partner. Of course, she knew this. By day two, my gifts—which I had taken two weeks to select, each geared for the most complex arrangement of psychological effects—were obviously from me. She knew it but didn't let on. And I knew she knew, but I refused to bring it up until she brought it up first. It was an intense non-dating relationship.

Everything was going okay at first. (I can admit now that I was embarrassing both of us.) But then, on Thursday, just before the climactic gift of the specially ordered Incredible Hulk lunchbox, filled with rose petals and chocolate-covered pretzels (long story), she left the Mogwai stuffed animal (Tuesday's gift) on the brick wall in the senior locker area. During second period, the stuffed animal—only about the size of my fist, really—had been knocked off the wall and trampled and was lying on the wet, sticky floor where I discovered it at Break.

I was coming out of Chemistry, and it just pissed me off to see it discarded like that, like some piece of trash. I'd gone to a lot of goddamned trouble to find that stuffed thing, and it had all kinds of precise emotional reverberations I wasn't about to spell out. I was picking it up when Melissa approached. She didn't say anything though, just stood there inspecting me.

"Just cleaning up your stuff," I said.

"Say what?"

"I'm just cleaning up your stuff."

"Well, I didn't put it there. It must have fallen," she said.

"Sure."

"Where else was I supposed to put it?"

"Oh, I don't know. Your locker. Your bag. Take it with you."

"I'm not going to take it with me. How weird is that."

"Then I don't know. Hell, just throw it away for all I care."

And with that I shoved the stuffed animal into her hands, but she just shoved it right back, saying, "I don't want your stupid gift."

I swear Melissa showed her teeth when she got angry, her upper lip pulling away so that she looked a little feral.

She turned and walked up the stairs, and as she escaped she had the haughty aura of someone obviously in the right who was dealing with a deranged person. At least, that's what I thought at the time. I don't know. She would turn her back and walk away from me, just completely discard me, whenever something didn't turn out exactly like she wanted. It just infuriated me.

I mean, understand: I was 17.

So anyway, I threw it at her, the Mogwai. It wasn't that hard really, except for the plastic eyes and nose. It flew amazingly straight, much more accurately than I could have predicted, and it hit her at the base of the skull. She was about midway up the flight of stairs at the time. She didn't fall but did have to clutch the banister with one hand and the back of her head with the other.

She spun around, her teeth bared, screaming, "What the hell are you *doing*? Are you crazy?"

And as I approached her, all apologies now, the anger having evaporated as soon as I threw the Mogwai, she jogged and then sprinted away, and the Mogwai was lost in the blur of all those feet getting to class.

But I still asked her to prom.

She was home during Spring Break and I went over there during the day and popped the question after about two minutes.

"Okay," she said. "I'll go."

Good, I said, and we continued to drink the lemonade she had been making when I arrived. It was sweet and cold and the slick glass felt good in my hands and the knot in my stomach began untwisting itself, thinking about how all of this—Stiph and SS, me and Melissa—was going to work out.

"Is that the only reason you came over here?" she asked.

"No. No. I wanted to ..."

"It's the only reason, isn't it?"

"No."

"You can leave, if you want. If you need to."

"I would like to stay."

"You've done your job."

"Do you not want to go? You don't have to."

"I know," she said. As she drank the lemonade, she seemed to bite the glass. I could see the liquid straining through her teeth.

"It'll be fine," she said. "I'm sure not going to go with anybody else at school," she said with an odd, short, hollow laugh.

I tried to laugh along. But I knew that she had been tentatively seeing this boy from another school in town. They had met, somehow. (I was never sure how people met kids from other schools.) She hadn't told me about it, but I knew. Jackson's not that big. Both of them were coming off of big breakups and were afraid of rebounding or something like that and were "taking it slow." I had heard that she really liked him.

If Melissa had a fault it was that her exhaustion with me was matched only by her pity. When I needed it, I knew that I could go back to her again and again and that she would never dry up. If we were both in good moods, we could get along fine together. If we were both just *there*, slugging along in another day, our relationship was like a chore, but I knew that if I came over feeling beaten down, that she would react accordingly and that her excitement and interest in me would be proportional. I've never met anyone quite as useful as Melissa.

She was wiping the bottom of her glass with a napkin and trying to force a smile.

"I should probably head on home," I said.

She nodded silently.

C8

Before long I was guilted into helping with prom prep. So on a Friday afternoon sometime in March, I found myself stuffing colored tissue paper into chicken wire. For the "A Night on the Nile" theme, we were making this gigantic sphinx about the size of a pickup truck. Yellow tissue as far as the eye could see. Sarah sat Indian-style in front of me, busily stuffing in perfectly proportioned fluffs of tissue.

"Are you going to the prom?" she asked.

"Do you think I would help out if I wasn't going?"

"I don't know. You could just be really bored," she said. "Or maybe you have a crush on Jessica."

This was an absurd joke. Jessica Hyne was the prom coordinator, the junior in charge of the whole shebang. Melissa had been the P.C. the year before and was now serving as the senior adviser, which meant she was basically JH's overlord, making sure she didn't foul the greatness she had established the year before.

"I don't think so," I said. SS leaned onto her knees to fluff the tissue into homogenized perfection. She wore the standard-issue navy blue cheerleader shorts, with the elastic waistband flipped inside out to make them even shorter. The words "Got Spirit?" were stenciled on the rear.

"Who are you going with?"

"Melissa."

"Oh. Are y'all back together?"

"No. We're just friends."

"Uh-huh. So do you still like her?"

"What? No. I said we're just friends."

"Mhmm. Does she like you?"

"I ..."

"Who's keeping you just friends? Is it you or her?"

"I think we're both—I'm sorry, what?"

"You like her. I can tell."

"No. I don't."

"Yes. You do. You're blushing. I can tell."

"No. We're just friends. I don't like her at all."

"Don't like who?" piped up a third party—another girl doing the poke and fluff a few acres of chicken wire to the left.

"Melissa We—"

"Nobody," I said.

I was sweating at this point, probably blushing. The third party sat waiting, wanting in on the talk. After a moment to let me squirm, SS scrunched her nose and shook her head. *Never mind, dear.* I felt like dabbing my forehead with the tissue. She cut a glance at me and grinned.

"You *do* like her," she hissed.

"Shut up and stuff," I said.

A few minutes later, after cooling down and regaining my composure, I said, "What about *your* date?"

"What about him?"

"Who are *you* going with?"

"You know that, dummy."

"Yeah." Suddenly, I regretted my sarcasm.

"Why did you ask?"

"I'm just messing with you."

"Don't poke fun."

"Are you excited?"

"Sure. I mean, yeah. I love the theme. And I think the pictures will be beautiful."

"No. About Jason."

"Jason's nice. I mean, it's nothing serious. It's just a date. But I think he's a nice boy."

"He is."

"I know. That's why I said yes."

"You wouldn't hurt his feelings would you?"

"Yeah, I'm going to run him over with his car."

"No. I'm serious."

"How would I hurt his feelings?" she asked, pausing with a burst of yellow tissue at her fingertips. It looked like a fake corsage. She stared at me. I thought I saw the beginnings of a blush creep up the base of her neck.

Finally, I said, "I don't know. I'm just messing with you."

"Who do you think I am?"

"Hey. I'm just messing with you. Just be nice to him, okay?"

"Why wouldn't I be nice to him?"

"Look, Sarah, it's not *you*, okay? It's just ... last year he got ditched."

"What?"

"I shouldn't tell you about it. It's like ancient history."

"What happened? Tell me."

"Nothing. Never mind."

"No, tell me."

"Last year. Okay, listen. But this is just between us. Last year, his date—this girl from like somewhere in Alabama—she didn't show up."

"Why not?"

"I have no idea."

"Was he like totally heartbroken?"

"No, he was fine. It's just that—"

"Well, I'm not going to ditch him. I said I was going to go."

"No. I know that. I was just—"

"Does he like have tons of hang-ups about prom now or something?"

"No. I just wanted to *tell* you. I just thought you should *know*."

"Okay."

"So just ... have fun."

"Oh, I will. Don't you worry about that," she said, stuffing and fluffing, stuffing and fluffing. "It's gonna be the bomb."

ೞ

When the night finally came, we had to get there two hours early so Melissa could advise the supposedly needy Jessica Hyne. I picked her up in plenty of time but she was livid and said we were running late, and so I drove like a madman out to the convention center while she put on make-up in the fold-down mirror and told me not to swerve.

When we got there she clacked away in her heels and I was left alone. There was the occasional spouse-in-training moment of helping to lift something or commenting on the decorations, but I soon opted for solitude and sat out back behind the building on the loading dock and smoked cigarettes and massaged my feet through the shiny patent leather.

Melissa was angry, probably about agreeing to go with me, but I couldn't care less because she was dressed in a silver-gray satin dress that fit her like eel skin. I had bought a corsage but it was still sitting in the backseat. This was all part of the deal, I knew. This was a non-date date. I hadn't gotten a call from Stiph while I was getting ready, but instead of calming me down it only made me more nervous about everything. I imagined him picking up the tuxedo, dressing slowly and with deliberate care, putting on those ridiculous white gloves only to drive over to her house, which by then would have somehow vanished, blown away by some mysterious wind.

If I'd had a cell phone back then, I probably would have called. Instead, I daydreamed apocalyptically and smoked while the sun set. After a while, I started taking sips from my flask. It was thin and silver and had a seal on one side, small and circular. The flask had been my grandfather's, and I was using it on a lark, trying to drink up the fifth of Jim Beam I had begged Ronald into buying for me. I think it was real silver, and it stayed remarkably cold, so that when I slipped it back into my tuxedo breast pocket, I could feel the rectangular metal coolness against the left side of my chest.

Before long the full, pockmarked moon was out, and the whole school was arriving in a caravan of honking. They pranced in, arm in arm, already fairly soused and practicing a kind of faux-elegance they had either picked up from their parents or the television. Then we were all on the dance floor and the black band, the same one as last year, was chanting *Hey Hey Hey Hey* as the lights glistened off their sequined jackets. The throng on the dance floor was split into three layers. Towards the back, people milled about tentatively, unsure if they really wanted to dance but wanting to be near the action. The second, middle layer danced with abandon, while the closest layer, pressed against the stage, was composed of girls who had discarded their dates to stare upwards at the band and sway out of time. In the back of the hall, people flew from table to table like bees traveling the honeycomb. I was all over the place. Every few songs, Melissa would appear and we would dance with the utmost of self-consciousness, and then she would remember something she needed to check on and would slither away, and I would dance alone for half a song until I felt weird, and then eventually I would float out of the orbit of the dance floor and try to mingle. I'm still not good at mingling.

Finally, deep into the second set, after the shoes and coats and corsages had come off and the scant faculty had retired to the dark recesses of the room to recline and ignore, I ran into Stiph. He could have been there for hours but he looked like he had just arrived. He was wearing his top hat and his white gloves and he even had a cane. SS was on his arm wearing a blue dress that seemed to be one large sequin. Her shoulders were bare and her hair was up and her long, pale white neck was exposed.

Stiph and I shook hands and chatted. He was ecstatic, I could tell. He took off his hat and fanned himself. His hair was pressed down in a dark, wet rim from the headband, but he didn't take off his coat or even his gloves and only briefly fanned himself with the hat before putting it back on.

"How's Melissa?" he asked.

"Huh?"

He repeated himself.

"Oh, she's fine. She's off doing stuff. I don't know. Administrative crap. It's like she's running the whole show. I just bump into her every once in a while."

"Is everything going okay?"

"Oh, yeah. I'm good. I ate before I came. The band's totally badass."

He patted me on the shoulder, his hand formless and soft in the white glove. I felt like I was being regarded by my butler. "We'll be on the dance floor if you need me." They walked off, her delicate bare arm hooked with his, her neck glowing in the soft chandelier light, her calves smartly revealed by the cut of her glittery dress.

CB

A little while later I found Melissa with a gaggle of her friends.

"Hey," she said as I approached. "I was just about to come find you."

"You wanna dance?" I asked. "I think their second set is about to end."

"Yeah. They're almost out of cups. We've got to book it to campus real quick and pick up extras."

"At campus?"

"Yeah. We should be gone about fifteen minutes. We could have brought them in before, but you know, we were late."

"Yeah. Okay. That really sucks."

"Meet up when I get back?"

"Oh yeah. I'll be here."

"Don't leave without me."

"No worries," I said, and then she and the girls walked off toward the bathrooms. I turned back to the dance floor. Through the limbs, I could see Stiph and Sarah dancing. He was twirling her. His cane was gone and his gloves had been taken off, but the top hat was still there. The song ended in an explosion of horns and Stiph dropped her hand and began clapping violently. He put his fingers up to his mouth and whistled—high, loud, sharp. The second set was over. He continued to whistle. It was a sound I had always disliked.

303

I went to the car and refilled my flask. The bottle was stuffed under the passenger's seat, and the corsage stared at me through its plastic box as I tried to pour without spilling. I slipped the flask back into my coat pocket, and I made my way back through the convention hall to the back loading dock where I had smoked earlier. It was still abandoned, dark, and quiet. I sat against the wall, which was strangely warm, and I took drinks every now and then and smoked cigarettes. Somewhere from off in the woods came the smell of pot. I smiled, realizing that I wasn't the only person away from the action.

The full moon glistened off the band's small trailer, and though they had quit briefly, I could still feel the movement of the people and the talking through the wall. I stayed out there until the third set started and the wall began to vibrate and I could no longer feel everyone's voices and footsteps. I decided to go back in. I wasn't trying to worry anyone by hanging out there. I stood up and took a moment to regain my balance. The loading dock and the band's trailer and the trees out beyond were all lit up now in the wet silvery light of the moon, as if I'd suddenly entered a negative film of my prom evening. I took out my flask for one last drink but it was all gone, and the flask was like a mirror held out to the light, gathering all of the moon's energy within it.

I found Stiph quickly. His face was ashen and I could see the sweat on his shirt, which had become almost clear with the moisture.

"Where you been?"

"Just outside," I said.

We meandered toward a table and sat.

"You seen Sarah?" he asked. I shook my head. "We were dancing and then suddenly everyone rushed the stage and we were all crammed together."

"You okay?"

"Yeah. I'm all right. She's probably peeing." He had also lost his hat, and his hair was now spiky from him pushing it off his forehead. His tie was loose and his jacket gone.

"You're probably right," I said. "Everything going okay?"

"Oh, yeah. Smooth sailing," he said. He was pulling a napkin out of its ring and spreading it out flat on the table cloth, smoothing out its wrinkles as he talked. "It's been totally great. The bomb."

He pressed the napkin with the palms of his hands, and then began to wipe his sweaty face.

"How long's she been gone?"

"Just a few minutes. It's no problem. She's probably in the bathroom," he said, now digging in the wicks of his eyes with the napkin, his glasses displaced by his fingers, riding up onto his eyebrows.

He finished with the napkin and readjusted his glasses and looked at me straight on. "Definitely my best prom yet," he said.

There was something in that moment. Even now, I still remember it vividly. I knew he wasn't telling me everything. I was sure there was something. Somehow the night hadn't fit with the dream he'd envisioned.

"Stay here and recuperate," I told him. "I'll go find the ladies." He nodded, still holding onto the napkin.

I found Melissa halfway down the length of the hall. She bolted out of the shadows, and I thought she was smiling but she was not smiling.

"Where the fuck have you been?" she said.

"I was just out back."

"Out back where?"

"Out back of the building. I was just having a cigarette."

"How many? Like a whole pack?"

"What does it matter? You weren't here."

"I've been trying to find you for like an hour. I thought you left me."

"I'm here. Ready and waiting." She sighed through her teeth and rolled her eyes, which were red, like she'd been rubbing them with her fists.

"We need to ride."

"What?"

"I'm tired, Peter. I want to go home. I've been wanting to go home for an hour."

"Then why didn't you tell me an hour ago?"

"I don't feel well," she said.

"Okay."

"I think I'm going to be sick."

"Right. Need a doctor?"

"I'm serious."

"Sure. You need to go home and 'puke,' right?"

"I've been feeling bad almost all night."

"Right. You want to go? Fine. Where's Sarah?"

"Who?"

"Sarah. You know, Sarah Samson."

"What do you want with her?"

"What do you think I want with her? None of your business what I want with her. I'm looking for her for Jason. Jesus. You're so fucking difficult."

Her face tightened up. Her eyes were bleary—maybe she was actually sick?—and her mouth was clasped shut and I knew that she wouldn't participate anymore that evening.

"Do you want to go home now?" I said. She shook her head. "Fine. Then you can go over and sit at our table over there. See Stiph? That's our table. I'll be back in a minute."

I moved to the bathrooms where SS was standing with her compatriots from the squad.

"Hello ladies. How's it going? Hey Sarah, what are you doing right now?"

"I was about to go to the bathroom."

"Oh no. Stiph and Melissa and I are about to dance and you should come."

"I will but—"

"Oh, come along," I said, reaching for her hands and touching them, pulling at her soft, soft fingers. "It's the last set and I think my date's gonna ditch me soon, so we gotta motor."

"I will. I will. But first I have to pee." She was giggling and turning away.

"Uhn. Whatever. Nobody ever wants to dance."

"I'll be right there."

"Better hurry. We don't sit well with liars."

"You okay, Peter?"

"Yes. Fine. Fine. Go pee. Have fun with your *eau de toilet*. With your bowhead friends. Don't slip and fall."

"What?"

She stood in profile, one shoulder flush against the restroom door.

"You know, break a press-on."

"Excuse me?"

"Nada."

"What did you say?" She was no longer giggling, had stopped smiling even. A few of her friends had made it into the bathroom ahead of her, but the rest swarmed around us.

"Well, are you going to pee or are you coming to dance because you sure as hell can't do both."

"What?"

"Too messy. Probably physically impossible, even. You understand, don't you?"

She leaned into the door. "Don't go too far," I said. "We know where you live. We'll huff and we'll puff and we'll blow your house down."

She spun around, her face mottled red, crimson flaring and receding like sunspots. Her face was quivering, her hair was slowly untying itself from the arrangement atop her head. She then mustered the harshest phrase she could possibly utter:

"Forget you, Peter."

The door to the women's bathroom swung closed and all I could see was the advancing and receding graphic of a woman in a triangle dress. I could feel Melissa at my shoulder. The door fanned in my direction, in/out. *I'm getting a ride home with Jessica*, she was saying. Fine. Fine. Off with you. In or out. The triangular woman on the door. *I can tell you're drunk and I wouldn't ride with you even if you weren't a total asshole. I didn't even want to be here.*

And then I was inside the bathroom. One girl was sitting on the counter trying to light a cigarette and another was standing beside her with her arms folded. A trashcan stood next to me with a large plastic-domed top. Sarah was standing next to the wall daubing at her eye with a folded corner of toilet paper. Her face was streaked with tears and the color had left her face except for a few ribbons of bright, embarrassed skin. It made her look like she had been attacked by a child with a magic marker.

"Get out of here," someone said.

"I don't care what you think of me," I said.

"Peter, what are you doing? Please get out of here," Sarah said.

"Your date is looking for you."

"Peter, please get out of here."

"He's been looking for you and I told you not to dick him over."

"I don't know what you're talking about. Please get out of here."

"I told you his history and you promised me you wouldn't dick him over so don't act like a little bitch and hang out in the women's bathroom all night."

"I have no idea what you are talking about. You're really scaring me."

"Don't kid me, Sarah. This is the perfect time to leave him. And if you do I swear to God—"

"Peter, you are so hopeless."

"I'm not the one hiding in the bathroom."

"Jesus, Peter. I'm not going to hurt your stupid friend."

She turned to walk to the back stall, and I said *don't you fucking go back there*, and I threw the rounded top of the trashcan towards her. It hit the side of the nearest stall.

Everyone said a variety of things to me then, but I only remember shouldering Sarah and forcing her on top of the trashcan where I began to try to stuff her down into the hole, and I could feel her kicking me—those strong calves coiling and releasing, and her nails, which were real, carving at my neck—and I was in that position, standing over her, my hands on her narrow, glittery gymnast's waist, pushing her into the trashcan, when Stiph pulled me off of her, and we fell back together onto the cold, damp, tile floor.

ᔆ

That was all nearly ten years ago. Back then, at that precise moment, everything I did made sense, had a certain amount of logic stuck to it. But now, all these years away from home, almost nothing makes sense. Apologizing now seems ridiculous.

I haven't seen Stiph, Sarah, or Melissa since graduation. Sarah, I hear, is still around Jackson. Stiph evacuated immediately after graduation and has not returned, which was to be expected. He needed some big state university where his talent for meticulous eagerness could find a proper outlet. Melissa went north to school and last I heard she was in some bitter live-in relationship with a guy stuck in graduate school. Which sounds about right, considering her talent for patience. I imagine her living in the hiply decrepit part of town and having a dog, wearing lots of scarves, and feeling trapped. I would like to see all of them, despite myself. They're not like my other friends, the ones close enough to check in on my mother when they're in town, the kind I get updates on when I manage to call home. They're like the friends you make at work. Intimate, but they don't know where you live. They don't know how you got here.

I've got this summer clerking job up in Atlanta, and I commute a long way every morning, which gives me plenty of time to think about how I've ended up where I have—in law school, six hours away from any family. I find the drive strangely soothing. Heading toward the city is like sliding down a long hill. For a few miles the interstate is several lanes wide. I often share those lanes with the semi-trucks. I used to be afraid of them, but I have grown used to them, even like them now. What I like most is getting in the center lane and being snug between two semis. They couldn't stop if they wanted to, and for a short few miles we run together, my car about midway down each of their long torsos. What I find most soothing is the height, the level of their wheels with my windows, and the way they speed so intently down the road, so captivated within their lanes while I travel along between them as if propelled along only by their proximity. I know that if they decide to change lanes without looking or if a car brakes hard in front of us, that my lane will be the swerve lane and I'll be crushed, but this threat of violence quiets me and stops the thinking and I turn down the music and roll down the windows and listen to the wheels spinning over the pavement, and I savor that moment before we are all released at the edge of the city and spun off to our separate destinations.

Every Good Boy Does Fine

End of the day, at the mailbox, my metal portal to the outside world. Every day it goes the same: I park in the little lot, leave the A/C running, and pry open the trap door. It's always stuffed with the same pseudo-adult crap—the credit card pitches, the free trial subscriptions, all those goddamned J. Crew catalogs. I bought one shirt last summer and now they just won't stop. And always there's a miniature mound of sand. It's not very much, sometimes just a pinch, but I'm always absently raking it out onto my shoes. I guess the apartment people thought it would be cute and, you know, tropical, to have a bunch of sand running from the mailboxes to the laundry room. They even dropped in those flat stepping-stones for a path, but now the sand has scattered everywhere, and the stones have slipped too far apart to actually use, and the dead yellow grass shows through. A shame.

Today it's more of the usual—bank statement, sand, water bill, sand, another free CD from AOL—except for this square, vanilla envelope. It's got my name handwritten in swirly cursive followed by "and guest." I don't recognize the return address. It's from somewhere out in Madison.

I rip open the envelope and it's a wedding invitation. It's got that slightly opaque wax paper-type stuff—like some scrap of preserved toilet paper—which crinkles and falls to the ground. There's the invitation itself which is in this kind of aggressively floral print, and then there's this little miniature envelope with a little miniature notecard, like the invitation's very own tiny reflection of itself. I study it and see it's my RSVP—am I like coming or what? So I finally read the invitation and it's for Jeremy and his girlfriend, Maddie Kennel, or as the invitation has it, *Miss Madison Anne Kennel, daughter of Dr. and Mrs. Robert Quincy Douglas Kennel of Lake Cavalier, Mississippi.*

I study the font some more. I study the wording (*would be honored by your presence*). I flip through the whole kit, the hey, we're getting married kit. It's eight weeks away. They've registered at Restoration Hardware. I study my response: *Will attend with _____ guests* or *Will not attend.* They only give you two options.

❧

My friends have entered the season of matrimony. I'm 27 now and the bells of their testicles have been ringing church hymns for a good three years now. I've been to so many of them I've stopped buying presents. Each time I'm back home for one we all sit around at the reception, sweaty and drunk, our tux shirts pasted to our backs, and we say, We never see each other except at these things. And then we sigh, take a drink, and crane our necks to see who's got the cigarettes. And then we go back to our various corners of the map to our jobs (or in my case, to my "education") and don't talk to each other again until one of these emissaries beckons us back home.

But Maddie. Really? Maddie? Can he really be that serious about Maddie?

She's nice, of course. She's perfectly nice. When I saw her last fall, she was definitely perfectly nice. But still.

It was Thanksgiving and for once we were all in town and there wasn't a wedding. Of course, it took us a couple of days to actually get together. There are always so many false starts, so many catch-up-with-you-later phone calls that once we all got together at Jeremy's house I was in shock. Everyone was in the same room: me, Jeremy, Tubbel, Anderson, and Daniel.

And of course his mother just loves it. She's all around us, fussing, all "Can I get you anything to eat?" Which in and of itself is kind of a joke because that house was completely snack-free while we were growing up. I guess it's because she was a piano teacher and she always had kids running in and out. Didn't want to feed the animals. She'd left a student in the piano room down the hall who kept shouting "every good boy does fine, every good boy does fine ..." while plinking random notes with each word. She rolled her eyes at the noise and continued to interrogate us about our jobs.

We were all around the island in the kitchen, and when we get together we're all back in our molds pronto. We're sort of like *Star Wars*. Jeremy is the Luke Skywalker, except not quite as childish. Maybe he's the Luke Skywalker of *Return of the Jedi*: quiet, determined, containing some haughty inner wisdom. Anderson is the Han Solo, all smirky smart-ass cowboy parody. Tubbel is the Chewbacca character, the towering sidekick. Daniel is kind of like the Millennium Falcon; he basically just drives us around, unless he's having a breakdown and then we have to start talking nice. And I am essentially Princess Leia, always wanting to be in charge or at least thought well of by those in charge.

Anyway, Maddie walks in and everyone says hey and jokes with her and generally coos around her because we know this is her first holiday with Jeremy's family. There's nothing like some foreign family's forced rituals to prove how most holidays should be cancelled outright.

We all sympathize with her because we sure as hell wouldn't want to be hanging with Jeremy's mom for a long weekend. We know she's grilled the poor girl senseless. But Maddie seems to be taking it okay. She's got a nice clear wrinkle-free forehead and a bob do that seems old school in an unironic way. She's super pale, but her face's Pollocked all over with freckles. She kind of just reminds me of a schoolgirl all over. Her ears grow real red whenever Jeremy's mom starts asking her questions and she's got this laugh that sounds like husky hiccups. Apparently, she grew up alongside us in good ol' northeast Jackson, started out at Niskayuna even, but moved to Arkansas and then went to Duke. Her father's an Episcopal muckety-muck and they moved away before high school started, which is probably why I don't remember her. For some shady reason they're having the wedding in Jackson because she "knows so many people here." Apparently, she's out living in the family's old lakehouse at Lake Cavalier, just by her lonesome with all those jet skis and life jackets. The great unmentionable is how Madison was until recently very married, and God knows we're not going to say anything about it. We can pretty much all tell it makes Jeremy's mom nervous as hell. Maddie stayed and chatted for a while and then disappeared back into the rest of the house. Jeremy's mom stuck around a while until Jeremy made some comment about her leeching and trying to relive her glory days and she got all blushy and *pshaw* and left. Her student was still pounding out the treble clef, and she scooted through the house, saying, "No, honey. It's E *G* B D F."

After she left we just stood there. Anderson was laughing at something but it was like he was trying to break the nervous silence.

"So Jeremy, she got you booking churches yet or what?" Anderson said.

"Not yet, man, not yet," Jeremy said.

And there was something in the way he said it that sent silent waves through the room. We could all feel it. We could all sense the lack of struggle in his voice, a kind of agreement, and we all knew right then that he was saying he's going to marry this girl, and he didn't even have to come out and say it. He just had to not deny it. You could see the understanding on everyone's face, the way they were reflecting Jeremy's own bemused half-smile—the kind of smile that's amazed at what it's gotten itself into.

Daniel articulated everyone's tacit approval when he said, "Well, she's a really nice girl."

In this plague of weddings my core group has been almost completely diminished. Tubbel's hitched of course, and Daniel's been married for like a freaking decade—some girl he goes to med school with. He's in the MD/PhD program at UMC and is trying to cure cancer, or something equally noble. Who knew Daniel would be our brightest star? Anderson's the most recent victim. He got married the previous spring to a girl I hardly know. I think she's a speech pathologist, but I'm not really even sure. I would know more about everything if we actually ever had enough freaking time to talk about any of it.

People used to bug me about it—the whole *When you gonna procreate?* question—but when my Dad died everyone pretty much shut the fuck up. Jeremy was always *the* catch of course. Whenever we bumped into anyone around town, the first person they asked about was him. So, what's Jeremy been up to? The female-to-male translation of this is: "Is he attached?" And of course there was always this bloom to their whole face when we reported that he had just broken up with Theresa, or that yes, he was still single, or that yes, he's *still* single and he's in law school. That got them opening like roses.

Theresa was his previous girlfriend, and I guess it has been a little over a year now since they broke up. She was the girl he was with pretty much through college and a little while after, the one we all basically thought he was going to marry. Even his mother had resigned herself. She was dark like his mom, all olive skin and thick hair and jungle eyebrows, but Greek where his mom was Italian. She had these super red sportscar lips, and when she drank she had this habit of burping incredibly loudly, like Homer Simpson-loud. One time she totally ripped one and his mom stormed in from a lesson (an angry version of "Pop Goes the Weasel" was playing overhead, I think) and she asked what all the racket was and said how godawful rude that was. We got all sheepish, but Theresa piped up and said she was real sorry with that killer smile of hers. His mom just adjusted her glasses and asked if Jeremy would make sure and take the garbage out, even though it was a Saturday and the garbage didn't go until Monday.

They were living together up in Virginia after college, and when I was in D.C., I used to go see them. This was not too long after my Dad died and I didn't really have time to go home and I didn't feel like having my mother come up and hang out. But still there was this need to, you know, be around people. So I would go up and stay with Jeremy and Theresa and they would take me to all the sights.

They were living in the lower half of this gigantic split-level house in Richmond. The owner of the top front half was this linguistics professor from the university who was divorced and otherwise alone and who seemed constantly amused at our youthfulness and faux-bohemianism. At night we would cook out on the back porch and he would show up and drink this really good import beer and generally just hang around us, mainly to hear how we talked.

"You know that when you use the word 'like' before you say something that you're really performing the words?" he would ask sometimes.

And we would just nod along and drink his beer and he didn't seem to mind, and eventually he would disappear back into his upper level and we would stay out as the grill cooled and smoke cigarettes and watch the activity in the well-lit houses behind the porch. We could see into the back kitchen windows of three houses, four if we walked out into the yard, and it was always interesting to see what happened as the night aged. It was better than TV. There was this one guy who didn't eat with his wife but took the meal she made for him (she was often cooking while Jeremy was cooking) and went into a computer room of some sort, where he sat in front of that blue screen all night. The woman would sit at the kitchen table and work on some paperwork, a crossword maybe, and every once in a while her head would raise up and we could tell that she was trying to talk to him. But those little conversations never lasted long and soon she would be busying herself with some other chore while we sat outside and clucked our disapproval between beers.

Sooner or later we'd have to go to bed, too. Theresa and Jeremy would be off to their own room and I'd smoke a few more cigarettes by myself, giving them time to get settled, and then I'd go crawl into my waterbed.

It sat out in the living room, and when I wasn't there they used it as a kind of daybed. It had been left by Jeremy's old roommate, this guy from Michigan named Troy who was crazy about rock climbing. He used to go on trips. He'd load up all of his gear in the back of his 4Runner and drive for days so that he could grip some rock face for a weekend and then talk about it nonstop the whole next week. Summer before their senior year he fell and broke like half the bones in his body, and part of his rehab was this waterbed, which he left when he moved to Australia.

"It seems like everybody's moving to goddamned Australia," Theresa said one night. We'd been waiting for some of their friends who didn't show, and there was this general feeling that Jeremy and Theresa were the last ones holding onto the city. I mean, it had been over a year since graduation, and most of their school friends had moved away to weird fancy places like Australia or New York or San Francisco.

Of course, some would have said D.C. was a weird fancy place, too, and there were the boys and girls from our hometown who moved to D.C. and got involved in politics in some way. Really, it's just the hometown network transplanted to a congressional office. They go up there and fetch coffee and fax shit for eight months and suddenly everyone in Mississippi thinks they've "made it" up in Washington.

Perhaps that's why I went up there—to get some of this D.C. good luck that seemed to be infecting everyone back home. I know it made my father happy when I moved, because it showed direction, he'd said.

Sleeping in that bed was alright, nothing to write home about. Above all it was extremely cold. Even with sheets over that plastic sack of water it was cold. I'd crawl on top of that thing and it would swish and swirl around me. It was like I was this big, sinking pylon or something. I'd hold onto my pillow and eventually the amniotic rocking would stop and I could fall asleep.

Perhaps the bed was what made me such a light sleeper up there. I wasn't sleeping all that great back in D.C., sure, but the slightest bump would crack my eyes open and that wave machine underneath me would start to working. For instance, I would always wake up when Theresa went to the bathroom, which always seemed to be around 4:15. She would shuffle into the bathroom and close the door and light would shoot out from the crack at the bottom and I'd be pretty much up and ready to go at that point. But I'd stay quiet and keep my eyes closed mostly because I didn't want to frighten her. She always wore the same sweatpants that she'd made into shorts, the hem hitting at mid-thigh all jagged like some psycho had gone after it with a knife. They were this sea blue. Maybe it was teal. She wore that and one of Jeremy's shirts that was all thin and ragged out. You could tell in the mornings that she was self-conscious without a bra on because while waiting on her coffee she would fold her arms up tightly underneath her boobs like some disappointed kid.

But when she woke up in the early morning, she had this routine. She'd go to the bathroom and then she'd go into the little kitchenette they had and have a glass of water. The funny thing was that she drank out of the faucet. During the day she never did this. They had one of those water filter pitchers and

Theresa and Jeremy were adamant about using it. "The water up here is shit," they would say.

But there she would stand, one hand bracing herself against the countertop, the other hand holding a glass half-full of tap water, which she'd chug. It was strange. Maybe she was sleep-drinking.

After she finished she would let out this dainty little water burp and amble back to the bedroom, her shirttail usually caught in the ropey waistline of her sweatshorts.

All of which is to say that Jeremy and Theresa, you know, they were really nice to me during that time. I came up a good bit, almost every weekend from like July on. And I'd eat their food and invade their lives and they didn't seem to mind. And now I'm down here and I wish they were near or at least within a day's drive or a short train ride or something because I'm starting my second year and it's still fairly business-like at school. I mean, I've got my law school friends and we hang out sometimes but it really feels like I'm in some professional limbo. It's like I'm a bull at the rodeo and right now I'm just in the pen, having that rubber band strapped around my nuts, just waiting to be saddled with some real life rider shit and be let out to start bucking. I don't know. I think if I had Jeremy and Theresa close by or even a good non-ghetto train station to take me somewhere more urban, I might not get so apocalyptic about everything. But when you've been on party manners with so many people for so long, it's hard not to growl a lot, which is basically a long way of saying I threw the invitation on my desk.

Let it molder with all the other offers I don't feel like looking at.

ఆ

As expected, my mother began calling. More so than our now-standard every third day. Just after my dad died, we went to talking at least once a day, sometimes more depending on how she sounded. It was a strange time. She insisted I go back to D.C.

"You can't just stop your life now. You've got to go back. It would make him proud."

Of course, I wanted to go back. It's not like I wanted to stay in Jackson and watch her walk around all bereaved, but these pronouncements always made me well up. When I got back to Washington and we were talking on the phone, it was better because I could cry by myself in my room, while on the phone or not, depending on how my day had been and what she was saying.

Gradually, we began to talk less—only once every evening—and now that it's been like two and a half years, it's only every third day and sometimes, when I'm really busy and haven't had the chance, only twice a week.

But now we're back to every day on the dot. She's worried about me because she knows the invites are out. She's "bothered" that I haven't responded. To her, this looks like two steps back, not two steps forward. The problem is she bumped into Tubbel's mom who had heard from Jeremy's mom that I hadn't yet sent back the reply card.

"You need to go on and mail it back to them, Peter. They've got to have a headcount. If they don't have a headcount, they can't do the seating chart. This is Jeremy's family, honey. They're going to have *tons* of people there. I bet you it's the better part of 500. They've *got* to have a good seating chart. They've got to order the china. They've got to get the numbers to the club. This is a serious deal. You're holding it up if you're not sending your card back."

"Mom, I seriously doubt I'm holding up Maddie Whatserface's wedding shindig."

"Peter, there's no reason to stall on this. Just send the card in. Paul and I have sent our card in. We sent it in the *day* it came. It's not that hard, Peter."

Paul, I should mention, is my mother's new beaux, though publicly they are just good friends. For some weird glitch of southern manners, it isn't yet kosher for my fair widowed mother to be gallivanting with a single man, though when she talks she's always conspicuously a "we."

"Mom, lay off, seriously."

"I'm not going to lay off. I'm not going to let you just forget about this like you do with everything else so that Mrs. Kennel has to accommodate you at the last minute. If I were you I would buy a decent calendar."

"What does a calendar have to do with this?"

"Look, Peter. I'm not trying to criticize, but it would really help, I think, if you had a calendar to prioritize when things must get done. This is one of those things that must get done ASAP, okay?"

"Mom. It's just a wedding. It's like a month away."

"Peter, I want you listen. Honey, this is the most important day in Jeremy and Maddie's life, and to think," and here is where the tears broke in, her voice shuddering under the strain of my waywardness, "to think that you would mess up that perfection. I know you're not doing it intentionally, but God, Peter, everything is *so* important, and if you just do the small pieces that you have to do and if everyone will do the small pieces they have to do then we'll have a perfect wedding, which is what everyone wants."

What do you say to this weeping mother, this happily re-in-love mother with her awful paternal memories and all this fucking mannered hardship? I don't remember half of our conversations, because when the tears start I just go on autopilot until I get to a dial tone and I can be alone and try to forget her voice. Yes, yes, a calendar, my 20-somethings for a calendar.

But seriously, how can you be honest with that? How can you tell that kind of mother, who's mostly now so oppressively happy, that the invitation is buried under the other solicitations and credit card swindles on my desk? Actually, that's a perfect place for it because they're the same damn thing. Wedding invitations and credit card deals are the same scam. They're deals built on potential (credit, love) that you're supposed to believe in and can't help not believing in because, you know, you're supposed to, and your mother's on the other end of the fucking phone telling you how proud your father would have been if you would just come home and see everyone and go to another goddamned wedding where someone else will chant the magic words that somehow makes them all grownup special.

଼ଽ

On those weekends, we'd grab lunch and head out to some sunny embankment along the James River. We'd find a grassy knoll and spread out a quilt and have a nice lunch, those plastic potato salad boxes taped down with their long, ribbon-like price tags.

One day—over Labor Day weekend, summer's dying cough—we went to a new spot, the boulder spot, so Theresa could climb the rocks like she'd done last September. It was this ritual she had at the start of each school year and Theresa was adamant about upholding the tradition. Jeremy simply called it the Rock Spot and mumbled that Theresa was basically obsessed with it.

We were rounding a blind curve when it came into view. There was a long, narrow stretch of almost chemically green grass and this scattershot assortment of large, gray boulders in the water, like the rounded pieces of a jigsaw puzzle that hadn't come together. We pulled off the side of the road, the right set of tires falling off the lip and sinking into the soggy grass.

"We grassed the shit out of it over here," I said when I got out of the car. There was a good six-foot streak of mud tailing the rear wheel.

"No biggie, Pete. Don't sweat it," Jeremy said.

"Do you think we should pull the car off the road some more?" I asked.

"Car's fine," he said. A car swerved by us, and I waited, tapping my finger on the sun-warmed trunk as they made their way down to the riverbank, Jeremy carrying a rolled-up blanket under his arm and a Frisbee in his hand, and Theresa holding the sack of groceries in front of her like a big, pregnant belly.

By the time I got there, she was already setting stuff on the blanket—pasta salad, fruit cups, a bucket of chicken breasts, a battalion of individually wrapped plastic forks. She was wearing this yellow bandana like some pioneer woman trying to keep the locks out of her face. She sucked in her cheeks and asked where the dill pickles went off to.

Jeremy had tossed off his leather flip-flops and was squinting into the wind.

"Don't you want to get your sunglasses?" Theresa asked.

"Oh, God, can we just eat already?" he said.

We chewed quietly and nobody talked about the creeping wetness that was slowly soaking through our blanket. We were determined to have a good time, though Jeremy had been sour all day. We had said for weeks that this weekend was going to be fun, not that all the others weren't fun, but that this one was going to be especially fun because it was the last weekend of summer and I wouldn't be coming up all the time in the fall and Theresa had finally landed that job as a data entry clerk at that payroll place and Jeremy had decided that he was going to really try and get a job. It was a sealing up of everything. All their friends—Zeke, Shelby, Lucas, Springer, Dawn—had pretty much all stopped visiting since they had either serious, full-time, be-there-at-8-a.m.-type jobs or they had gone away. But like every time you say you're going to have fun no matter what, it never turns out to be *really* fun. And I had this feeling that I was somehow in the way that weekend. I mean, they were so nice to me that summer but I still resented the stiffness.

Of course, I knew what the stiffness was about. Jeremy's father had called a few days ago with a job for him, at home in

Jackson. It was a spot as a runner in his firm downtown, a good way for him to see the business. He'd been talking at various epiphanic drunken moments about how he needed to shape up and find the right track. He mentioned law school, though we pretty much all had, all of us who could only imagine a law career as a means of resolving some sort of subconscious economic melody in our heads, composed by our parents, which of course we were totally trying not to hear. Since graduation, Jeremy had had even less career success than me, working three or four nights a week as a valet for a swanky restaurant.

He told me about the offer that Friday night after he'd picked me up from the train. Theresa was in the shower, absently humming the refrain of some song. The door was cracked and steam poured forth and her thin voice floated over us as Jeremy whispered loudly, "I haven't told her yet."

"Well, are you?"

"Well, yeah. Duh. Of course."

"Right."

"I'm just not sure when."

"You going to take it?"

"I don't know. I'm thinking it over. It's an option."

Of course, we both knew that his father's offer was also an ultimatum. In the year-plus since graduation, Jeremy had learned he couldn't live as a valet, at least not in the way we were taught to live.

"I think you should talk to her," I said. He nodded but wasn't listening. He had that distant look he gets while watching TV. He got that look whenever Theresa was trying to tell him something important, and I couldn't help but feel I was betraying her somehow just then.

It was time to play Frisbee, Jeremy said, so we spread out along the thin strip of grass and started to hurl it back and forth. Normally we did tricks but that day we just threw plain.

Theresa put our picnic equipment away. She was still in her bandana but had taken off her shirt and her flip-flops, so was in her bathing suit and some grey gym shorts—just a regular blue one-piece, nothing special—and the grass had left two wet blurs on each buttcheek. She was going to the boulders, she announced. She had folded all of her things and placed them neatly on top of the nearest shore rock. From my position I could keep a good eye on her. But Jeremy had his back to her and nothing to look at but me and the Frisbee and the road behind us.

The boulders rose out of the water by a good three to five feet each. They were like gigantic prehistoric eggs of some sort. Theresa would reach the peak of one boulder and stand bent at the waist, her knees pinched together, her arms held out to catch her balance, then she'd squat down on the crest of the boulder like some mother hen and plot which rock to conquer next. Then she'd slide down into the shallow muck and wade over to the next rock.

The rocks speckled the shallow greenish-blue river and ran across to the opposite bank. There must have been thirty of them. The longer we threw the Frisbee, the further out she got.

Jeremy was usually a pretty good throw but that day he was all over the place. He kept throwing those short little dying shots where I had to run up and almost dive to get it. Needless to say I didn't dive. I just jogged and lunged right at the last second.

Before long he threw it hard left, and stumbling to get it, I almost ran into a cop.

"Watch out, son," he said as he side-stepped me. I performed this awkward combination of a stagger and a double-take and it took a good four yards for me to straighten myself out. He stood with his arms crossed, eyeing me like I was some retard.

"That your car up there?" he said. He was about my height with a tight chest and a face so clean shaven it looked lacquered. He couldn't have been much older than Jeremy and me.

"No," I said.

"Well, whose car is it?"

I leaned down and picked up the Frisbee.

He turned back to the river and to Jeremy, who was standing with his hands on his hips, squinting at the both of us.

"That your car up there?" the cop asked.

"What's it matter?" Jeremy asked.

"We got a lady says she nearly wrecked because of some Honda Civic out in the middle of the road."

"She oughta watch where she's going," Jeremy said.

"You got an attitude issue, sir?"

"Not until about two minutes ago."

I was petrified. I stood there with the Frisbee. By now the cop had gotten to Jeremy.

"I'm thinking that's your car up there," the cop said.

"Brilliant."

"Hey," I shouted. They both turned to me, but I was lost— no words to pull me through, nothing. So I threw the Frisbee, right at them. The cop stepped to the side and it slid into the soggy ground in between them.

"You throwing that at me?" the cop said.

"No. No. No. I was just ..."

"What are you *doing*, Peter?" Jeremy said.

"I don't know."

"Jesus," he said.

They both stared at me, baffled. I started to walk toward them.

"You should watch where you throw things," the cop said, and the shame burned through my face and my arms. "Why the hell you boys out here on a Sunday anyway?"

"My girlfriend wanted to climb the rocks."

We all turned to the river and saw Theresa, a blue speck on the top of a distant rock. Her head kept swiveling back and forth as if she couldn't decide which direction to go next.

"Right. Girlfriend."

"You know, we're just hanging," said Jeremy. "Enjoying the weekend before another manic fucking Monday."

"Manic Monday, right," said the cop in a flat robotic way that made me think he knew Jeremy was being some weird passive-aggressive smartass.

"Exactly," said Jeremy.

"So what're you, students?" asked the cop.

"No, man," said Jeremy. "We're having some fun before getting back to the salt mines tomorrow."

"Uh-huh. Dispatcher said a bunch of students parking their car in the road, playing Frisbee."

"We're not students," said Jeremy.

"Right. So you're—"

"Jesus. I don't know. We're just people. We're just grown up people having some goddamned fun," Jeremy said.

"Right, okay. So you grown-ups going to move your car or what?"

"Fine," Jeremy said, though he didn't move, only kept watching Theresa study the river and the rocks.

"C'mon, Jeremy," I said, picking up the wet Frisbee. "Let's get out of here."

We three began tromping back up the small incline to the two cars—Jeremy's black Civic and the cop's squad car, its lights strobing over the grass like a discotheque. The cop stood and watched Jeremy unlock the doors. I thought maybe the cop was going to say something really sarcastic since we were leaving and it didn't look like he was gonna give us a ticket, but instead he just stood there blank. He didn't even care enough to deal with Jeremy's attitude. So we climbed in and cranked it and waited for the cop to drive past us. He got maybe five hundred feet down the road when Jeremy hit the gas hard and the wheels spun out. I could see mud shooting out beside my window and the squad car hit the brakes, and I just knew he was about to swing a U-turn.

"Jesus, Jeremy."

"Don't fucking Jesus me," he said.

Finally, the Civic skipped onto the road and we began to limp away, mud thumping the fender as we picked up speed.

"Where you taking it?" I asked.

"Huh?"

"Where you taking it? How far?"

"We're going home, Pete."

"Home? Home-home?"

"What other kind of home is there?"

"But what about Theresa?"

Jeremy made some sort of non-committal shrug and pushed in the cigarette lighter.

"Jeremy, you can't just leave her out there."

"It's not like I'm leaving her in the friggin' wild," he said.

"Come on. Stop the car."

He didn't.

"Really, let's go back."

He kept driving.

"Come on, Jer, let's not do this. She's going to worry. This is really not good for the relationship."

The cigarette lighter thunked out and Jeremy plucked it from the console.

"I'm serious. Pull over. I'm getting out."

"Peter," he said, lighting a cigarette.

"I'm not kidding."

"Quit being so dramatic."

"I'm serious as a heart attack, man."

And then I opened the door. The white line on the side of the road was racing by, along with the mesh of gravel on the shoulder.

"Close the goddamned door," he said.

"Pull this thing over or I'm rolling," I said.

He yanked the steering wheel and soon we were bouncing off the road and skidding to a stop in more wet grass. The door slammed shut, rattling me back into my seat, and I generally lost whatever aura of cool determination I had somehow built up.

"You getting out now?" he said.

I managed to open the door and slide out. We might have been a quarter mile away from where we'd started, the cop nowhere in sight. Theresa, a blue-grey blob on the water, had turned and was wading back to shore.

Then, we started racing. Jeremy's car snorted past me as I went from a fumbling trot to a jog to a sprint. I don't know why I was racing him. The car had long passed me and was getting closer to the clearing, but I kept running. I was determined to beat him back.

I was panting and soaked. Wet mimosa branches hung low over my head like girls drying their hair and I shook free a new waterfall with each step.

And for some reason, I was still holding the Frisbee.

By the time I got there, Jeremy's car had pulled completely off the road and spun around on the field of grass, its nose staring me down as I hobbled up towards them. Theresa was sloshing to the bank from the last rock, her legs speckled with river grime. She had a kind of desperate ecstatic expression on her face, as if she had just won some sort of bet with herself. Jeremy was leaning against the car, staring at the shoreline, his arms folded, the cigarette smoldering from one of his buried hands.

"I'm whooped," Theresa said. I was approaching them, completely out of breath. "Y'all ready to go home or what?" Her forehead was glistening in beads of sweat, the bandana still tied over her hair. The tips of her shoulders shone red with fresh sun.

"Sure thing, babe," Jeremy said. I couldn't speak. I shook the Frisbee at her, a kind of wave I suppose, and Theresa reached down, grabbed her clothing, and began to stab her feet into her slick flip-flops.

"Would you?" she asked, indicating the sack of half-eaten food and the blanket. I jiggled the Frisbee again at her, indicating that I would help out, and I started to stagger over to what was left of our picnic.

On the way back to the house, she wouldn't shut up about the river, about the rocks, about how far apart they were and their height and width and projected mass. Apparently, she'd done some report on them back in school, and she was now something of an expert. She said that she'd never made it across like that before. She said she'd tried but had always gotten too scared, bored, or tired.

"That's cool, babe," Jeremy said.

She didn't say anything about our return, or Jeremy's crazy tire-donut he left in the grass, or my panting dash back to the river, or the cop or anything. Perhaps she didn't see it. I don't know. She just kept talking about the river and its boulders.

"You know they're getting father apart? Really. They are. Researchers have been testing it. They know they're moving; they just don't know why. Three-eighths of an inch each year. Some people say they can't tell, but I can. I swear. I haven't tried to cross since last fall and they definitely feel farther apart. Seriously."

"That's cool, babe."

I couldn't respond. I was out of breath for the rest of the day.

But it doesn't really matter. Whatever I could have told Jeremy or Theresa about their relationship was voided by their break-up a few weeks later. I wish I hadn't seen it coming. During the interim, I had felt distant, not sure what we were (friends? loosening acquaintances?) so I had merely put in the bare minimum as far as contact was concerned, a call once a month, maybe.

By the time he called to give me the news several months after, I was already set to move to Florida for law school so his new disposition was lost on me. I think he could feel this over the phone. All I could give him was the rote response. That really sucks, I can't believe it, y'all were so good together, how's working for your dad working out? He had found her without me and he was going to have to lose her without me. But none of this really matters, because now he's got Maddie, to have and to hold.

℣

It was probably a week before the wedding when Jeremy called. My mother had continued to rail against me just about daily, and then, about two weeks out, she stopped altogether. I got the plane ticket in the mail maybe a couple of days later, no note attached or anything, and quickly tossed it onto my desk.

Though my apartment is small, I like to let the phone ring for a while before I pick it up. I like the anticipation, wondering what the person calling is thinking, while my phone ring ring rings. I've got caller ID on the handset and it's nearly impossible not to look and then imagine what the speaker's doing while I pretend not to be home. Like when my mother calls, it always has my father's name because she was too lazy to change it. Or something. And I know she's just sitting in her bedroom scanning through the channels wondering where the hell I am. But then it rang about 7:30 one night with his mom's name still attached: Evelyn Moultas.

"Peter? Traxler?" Jeremy said.

"Hey, man. What are *you* doing? You home? My caller ID says your mom's calling me."

"No, just me. I don't know where she is. At the store, I guess."

"She still teaching?"

"Oh, yeah. She's got a new batch with school starting. They're all real cute, learning like 'Chopsticks' or something."

"Glad I don't have to listen to that all day."

"Yeah, she's got ears of steel by now."

"You're not living at home now, are you?"

"Oh, God no. I'm just over here dealing with wedding crap. Thought I'd give you a buzz. We're dealing with flowers now. The lady said she'd get us calla lilies and now she says she ain't got any calla lilies. You know how it goes."

"Bummer."

"Yeah," he said.

Then, silence, a whole rest.

"So," he said, "what's this I hear about you not coming to my wedding?"

"I never said I wasn't coming to your wedding."

"Really. That's what my mom said. I think your mom talked to her. She called maybe a week ago or something. I don't know all the details. They say you're not coming."

"No, I never said that," I said. "I never said that at all."

"Okay. My bad. So, then ... you are coming?"

I have a bad habit of pacing around the apartment while talking on the phone. It's a studio, and I keep the phone on this little table next to my recliner, right in the middle of the room (I call it the center of my universe) and I tend to pace the perimeter. By this point I had made maybe six laps. I tend to go faster, depending.

"Jeremy. To be honest, I don't remember what I said. My Mom's been razzing me real bad and I just was trying to get her to lay off. She's been real crazed since all that stuff with my Dad and all, and I just—I don't really remember to tell you the truth."

"I understand. That's cool. No sweat. I just wanted to touch base, you know."

"Yeah, I know. I know."

"I mean, we hadn't gotten your invitation card back and Maddie kept asking. You know how girls get before the big day. Scary."

"Oh, yeah. I understand, totally."

"But you did get the invite?"

"Yeah. Yes, I did. It's somewhere here in all my junk. School has been totally crazy lately."

"Yeah. So look, are you going to come? Maddie and I really want you to be there. I mean, that's why we invited you. I mean, we've invited tons of people—from school and everything. Maddie's got damn near half the state coming to this thing."

"That's great, man. That's really, really great."

"But I still want you to be there. All y'all, Tubbel, Anderson. I even invited Daniel with no prodding from Mama. I mean, is this about not asking you to be a groomsman?"

"What? No. No."

"I mean, I wanted to. Seriously. But the cathedral's so small. And Maddie's mom sort of kept us to five people each. And I've got my Dad as my best man, and Tubbel and Anderson are there, but you know I had to fit some of Maddie's family in there or she'd have a cow. So it's her two brothers and my brother, and I didn't mean anything by it. You know I think all that wedding party stuff is total bullshit."

"Oh, that's fine. That's totally fine. I really have no problem with that."

"See, I thought so. I told Mama that. I told her you didn't care. It's a pain in the ass more than anything, with the tux and all that."

"Oh yeah, totally."

"But I'm serious though. You really should come. It'll be great. We'll have way more time to hang out than at Anderson's wedding."

"Yeah, no I understand, dude. It's just ... I don't know what the deal is. It's just when I got the invitation, I got to thinking."

"Yeah?"

I was standing near my door at this point. I was kind of buried into the corner between the wall and the steel door, which is very cool if you put your bare arm up against it.

"I don't know. I was just thinking about us and everything, about how everyone's getting married."

"We're dropping like flies," he said.

"Yeah, and I was just thinking about that summer in Richmond. Remember when I used to come stay with you and Theresa, on that waterbed?"

"Yeah. Of course I remember that," he said, his tone changing, everything slanting to minor.

"I was just thinking about all the shit we did. I mean we mainly just hung out but I swear, thinking about it down here, it just seems so fucking fun. It just seems like such a good time, and I just—am I wrong? Do you see what I'm saying?"

"Yeah, no, you're right. It was lots of fun."

"Yeah. I mean, that's good, because I've been feeling like I've been going crazy down here thinking about that so much, and Theresa, I mean, what happened to her? Do you ever talk to her?

"No, Peter. I have no idea where she is."

"See, that just kills me. It just seems like if that was so great and fun, then why is it so like irreversibly just, you know, over?"

"I don't understand."

"It's just so over. It's just so, I mean, it feels like it was so long ago, but it wasn't."

"Yeah, I know what you mean."

"And I just miss it."

"I know what you mean, man."

"And I just miss her."

"Yeah, I know what you mean," he said, the same rhythm, the same beat.

I think by now I was probably crying. I don't really remember the last time I cried in front of anyone except for my Mom but that doesn't really count. And I don't know what started it, but I couldn't help it. I had stopped pacing, and I was just kind of squatting in that corner in between the cool door and the wall, sort of hugging my knees, and I just had to stop talking for a second.

"You okay, man? You okay?" he said.

"Yeah, I'm okay. I'm sorry, J. I don't really know what I'm trying to say. I don't really know what I want to tell you."

"It's okay, man. You don't have to tell me anything. Just tell me you'll come to the wedding. Just tell me that."

"Okay. Yeah, okay. I'll be there."

"Seriously?"

"Yeah, I can do it."

"That would be so great man. That would be so great to have you there and everybody."

"Sure, yeah. Everybody will be there. All the guys. It'll be great to see all of the guys."

"Oh yeah, Peter. Most definitely. It's gonna be the bomb."

After a few minutes we hung up, and I felt mostly good about everything. But I didn't get up from my spot. I just stayed crouched there, in that crevice. I thought about maybe going outside, taking a walk, but I knew the next call would be coming soon. It was inevitable. That door was so cool against my arm and my face, better even than air conditioning, so much cooler than that Florida sun outside, always so hot and unfriendly. When I open the door at the end of each day, when my bag's cutting into my shoulder and the mail's sliding out of my hand, it always makes this satisfying suction sound, like everyday I'm breaking some seal over and over again.

Then, maybe two minutes later, or maybe it was ten, or twenty, the phone rang again, and I knew it was her. She's already heard. What do you mean you're coming—this is so wonderful—I'm so proud—fabulous! I've left the small town, but the small town always moves with me, hidden somewhere inside, indestructible. The phone just rings and rings.

The receiver in my hand comes alive with the incoming call, lighting up green, and there's the number, and his name— Edward Traxler—my dead father. He would be so proud.

Reunited

"Peter? You there? You busy? Can I swing by?"

From his second floor apartment Peter watches Tubbel's truck pull into the lot across the street, his familiar blond head visible under the windshield. Strange that he now sees Tubbel more than anyone else, Peter thinks, as if seeing him made up for not seeing anyone else. Tubbel was like a hometown almanac. He knew everyone's location, number, occupation, net worth, approximate earning potential, and their history, both pre- and post-Niskayuna High. This databank of a brain was both exhilarating and oppressive, like Tubbel was the host of a quiz show about Peter's life. Below, Tubbel fiddles with something in his car. It begins to rain.

Seeing Tubbel like this is like a form of state-sponsored interrogation, Peter thinks. Suddenly a representative from the fatherland is in your domicile, asking questions.

The first few minutes they do small talk. He's been up in Missouri at a conference and he keeps stretching and yawning theatrically, saying he's been in the car so long his ass is raw. He asks Peter how the studying's going, says it sucks real bad about the Bar.

"So are you going to like practice up here?" he says, meaning Memphis.

"Yeah, I guess," Peter says.

"Did you come up here because it's easier, or do you have to like take it here if you want to be in Tennessee?"

He says this completely straight, honestly curious, honestly ignorant. His questions have none of the laced apprehension that Peter's mother's questions have.

"Well, I knew I'd have to take it again," Peter says, "and really I'd just gotten tired of living in Florida. So hot."

"Yeah, I hear you. I'm hoping we can get closer, too."

Tubbel and his wife have lived all over because of his research: in Louisiana, Texas, briefly out in Colorado, and now over in Georgia, studying up on the Okefenokee Swamp, something to do with the tannin in the water.

The fact that Tubbel is completely unfazed by or unaware of Peter's professional limbo embarrasses Peter even more than his mother's routine condescension, though he hides it either way. Peter knows his mother has been feeding bits of his recent biography to Tubbel's own mother. He's just not sure how much editorializing has trickled down. But surely Tubbel knows the basics, that Peter graduated from law school last May in Florida and promptly failed the summer bar and that now he's living in this apartment in Memphis two miles from his old college, studying for the next Tennessee bar, switching geographic states in hopes of switching some other state.

"So if you want to be closer to home, why didn't you just go back to Mississippi?" Tubbel asks.

"Well, I don't know if I really want to go back to Mississippi, you know. I just wanted to relocate."

"I get you. Try out a new place. Do you still have friends here from Sutchfield?"

"Some have stayed in town, but mostly not," Peter says.

They stand in the kitchen and Peter hopes the girl keeps quiet. There's gentle music coming from his bedroom's cracked door but Peter's fairly sure he can play that off as his regular study music.

Tubbel's going on and on now about their friend Anderson, how he and his wife Martee are in couples counseling but doing okay, and how all of that is kind of a big secret back home, but how Tubbel thought Peter would still be interested. Peter is staring at the Good Shepherd postcard on his fridge and hoping

Tubbel hasn't noticed it. Everything else incriminating seems to be out of sight: the girl and the pipe and the rest of the gear stashed in the bedroom, the air freshener expelled, the room fairly moderately domestically a-okay.

But the Good Shepherd postcard is indeed still stuck to his fridge. He had to forget something apparently. The card was an invitation for their ten-year reunion at Niskayuna later that month. (Wasn't it later on in the month? Or was it for early next month, since this month is almost over already? How long has that thing *been* up there?) Peter wasn't totally sure why he'd kept it. He was adamantly against going, despite whatever his mother said. He just seemed to have a hard time throwing the right things away lately.

The Good Shepherd was this statue in the quad at Niskayuna High. Back then it was just one of those anonymous campus objects stuck inside your school day, but now—photographed and printed out and mailed back to you—it was immediately transformed into this artifact of your own adolescence, a little engine of nostalgia.

Tubbel's now on to Betty Benson, whom he recently ran into in the Atlanta airport. Tubbel's always running into people. He's practically magnetic.

"She's doing her residency in Chicago," he says, "and God, she's still gorgeous. Still totally stacked. She said she's getting married next April—some guy she met kayaking in Alaska. She's still totally into that. Did you ever do Outward Bound?"

"No."

"Yeah. I always kinda liked the idea of bathing, myself. Whew."

"What kind of doctor is she going to be?"

"A neonatologist."

"Fancy."

"Yeah, no joke. Hey, do you remember that time when she farted out on the quad?"

"I think so."

"That still kills me. She's still super sensitive about it."

"Did you ask her about it?" Peter says.

"No. Not really. I could just tell."

And Tubbel dissolves into giggles at the memory. Peter wants to feel superior, but he remembers, too. It must've been spring because they were all in shorts, sitting Indian-legged. Rising up for class, Betty let out a small, short, crisp, unmistakable fart, and any high school guy within hearing distance obliterated themselves with laughter. It was just so goddamn funny. Betty, her face a sun spot, ran to class. Afterward, she was still around, early afternoon, but of course word had spread and when people started kidding her, she slugged the nearest guy—she was a tomboy in spirit—and headed straight to her car and cut out early. It was all just so ridiculously funny, Peter remembers. This was back before the relative libertinism of college when the sounds and manifestations and procedures of female bodies were much more occult. And Betty's own body had always been worth studying. Ridiculously over-developed, cartoonishly curvy, Betty was a neurotic and single-parented 16-year-old stuck inside the shape of a girl from an old cigarette ad. She was pretty much a wreck and had snakes as pets. Peter wondered what she looked like now. His father'd always told him that girls inevitably turned into their mothers and he silently measured every girl he'd met this way. But Betty's mother was gone, supposedly crazy, institutionalized. There was no way to predict her. So for Peter, Betty was stuck as she was at graduation, like so many of his acquaintances from Niskayuna, whatever disproportion of body, state of hair, condition of skin, whatever psychological radioactive baggage they emitted. They were all still stuck, forever cropped, their images growing ever more lurid and bitmapped with repeated resizings from his memory.

He wonders suddenly if she still wears bras that snap in the front. He'd heard that about her. It seems like such a wonderful thing to remember about someone.

"Yeah, so speaking of which," Tubbel was saying. "Mary and I've got some news. Some big freaking news." He's laughing nervously.

"Yeah?" Peter manages.

"We're pregnant," Tubbel says.

"No shit? That's wonderful. That's amazing," Peter says, his brain windmilling.

Tubbel's face spreads into a blushy smile, like his pride is this gift that's just been unwrapped.

"Yeah," he says, "we're pretty stoked."

"When's she due?"

"At the end of March. Yeah, we just got back from the doctor like yesterday. Here," he says, pulling out this envelope from his back pocket, "check these out. I'm thinking of taking them to the reunion. Mom says she thinks everyone'll want to see. You're going, right?"

Peter takes the picture and it's from the ultrasound. At first he just tries to hold it correctly. It's like peering at a ghostly daguerreotype, white lines blurred under liquid, but he finds the baby. It seems impossible that this could be a baby—Tubbel's baby—and he thinks it irresponsible that doctors so blithely thrust this info onto all these gestating, would-be parents. Wouldn't it be better not to have these larval images? Shouldn't the parents and the baby all be kept in the dark? Everything more simply concealed underneath the belly. Sometimes this is just too much info to deal with.

"Here. These are the hands," Tubbel is saying. And suddenly out of the lightning-storm mass that is the picture a bone outline of a hand is there, next to the rounded globe of the head, a tiny balloon of white.

"It looks like he's lifting his hand to his face," Tubbel says.

Peter looks to Tubbel, jolted by the pronoun.

"I mean, we don't know for sure yet," Tubbel says. "But I just kind of can't help calling him a he." For an instant Tubbel's eyes go glazed with emotion, but they both swallow it and go back to the picture, so nothing major happens.

But to Peter, Tubbel's presence suddenly becomes distinct. He's no longer just Tubbel, king of fart jokes and snot bubbles and endless high school trivia. He's standing in a suit, bedraggled from travel, his tie loosened at the knot, sloppily professional, routinely professional, his blond stubble showing in certain light, the hairs like the dusting of sugar grains. How could Peter not anticipate this? Tubbel's become a variation of a grown man.

"So you're coming, right?" Tubbel asks, meaning the reunion.

"I can't."

"What do you mean you can't?"

"I mean, I've got to be here. I've got things. I've got to study."

Tubbel makes a face.

"Come on. It's not until what—February?" he says.

"Well I didn't exactly do so hot last time," Peter says.

"Well, it's like five months away. It's not like one weekend home is going to slay you. Besides, I know your mom would love to see you."

Peter thinks that the second worst part about going home now is having to spend so much goddamned time with his mother's boyfriend, Paul. The worst part is that his mother is so obviously happier.

"I just don't think the reunion thing's for me," Peter says.

"Why not? Come on. You have to be curious. We haven't seen these people in ten years. Don't you want to see what Betty looks like?

Peter is silent.

"Look. Let me have a drink," Tubbel says, turning to the fridge.

ಞ

Peter can see it all in his mind, how the reunion would play out. His mom's already been ragging him about it like always. She keeps saying, "but you love seeing all your old friends," but she's got it all wrong. She doesn't understand how many extraneous people would be there, how crowded everything would be. It's hard enough getting any good talk accomplished when you've got the exact people you want to have around, much less the whole goddamned class. *It's complicated*, Peter tries to explain. *How complicated could it be, Petey?* she says. *Niskayuna is just different,* he says back, shuddering at what he's said. He's heard other people invoke this same line—the Niskayuna Exceptionalism Clause—and he despises it because it's so horribly elitist and self-congratulatory and dumb, but he still uses it every once in a while, when he's in a conversational bind with his mother or he's out somewhere socially and trying to explain some finer point of his upbringing.

Going to Niskayuna was just different, makes you different. (He's said this out loud to people.) *Niskayuna's one of those schools where you spend every last minute there bitching about how much it sucks and the rest of your goddamned life talking about it, as if it's just the greatest place ever, though you would never actually say it was the greatest place ever.*

He's said this to girls he was trying to sleep with.

"Well why wouldn't you want to go to your 10-year reunion?" his mom says.

"I just don't want to see all those people, okay?"

"Well why not? You love seeing everyone when you come home for the weekend. At Jack Tubbel's wedding you couldn't wait to go out and see everyone. You hardly even came home all weekend. I don't understand."

"Mom, that was like two years ago or something. It's just different."

"How's it different? It's just more people."

"Well more people make it more complicated."

"What's so complicated? You go with your friends. Have a beer. Catch up with everyone. Take a date even."

"Mother, I'm so not taking a date to my high school reunion."

"Fine, then meet someone there."

"Mother, everyone's either married or a freak at this point. You know this."

"Peter, your father and I loved going to our reunions. Each one was a ball. You get to see how everyone turned out. It's fun."

"But I don't want to see how everyone turned out."

"Why not? Your father was always so fascinated by how people ended up."

Peter can see them now, everyone, all the guys standing with their weight on one hip, one hand holding a napkin-wrapped drink, the other stuffed deep into a pocket, shuffling keys. They stare off into space, talk about work, but euphemistically. So what are you up to now? And of course they talk about school. Do you remember that time when? The dweebs and the jocks will suddenly be reunited and the people you couldn't fucking stand back in high school will now somehow seem your equal, united in nostalgia. They seem really to care what happened to you after you got that B.A. in whatever.

And the women stand with their cocktail glasses just under their chins while they bob their heads back and forth to whatever

Sarah Samson's reporting. She still says "Ohmigosh, y'all" without any hint of self-awareness. And of course this all comes after the repetitive female chorus of "Oh, you look so *cute*" that reverberates throughout the quad.

Because of course they'll all be standing outside, in the courtyard, in that little area next to the Good Shepherd. It's the place where Susanne Rochelle always took a nap after lunch on that hard, gravelly concrete. When she woke up, she always had that pockmarked texture on her cheek, shoulder, outer thigh, like she'd been attacked with a pizza roller. But she was weird anyway, graduated a year early and never called you back, so fuck her.

The Good Shepherd statue looms in the background. Did anyone every really know what it was made of? Wood? Plastic? Metal? Burnt rubber? It's this skinny charcoal-gray sculpture of a man with this lamb on his back, draped over his shoulders, the legs hanging down. Surely welded or molded or cast by some alum from days gone by. He's on a little pedestal, bent over in the middle of a great journey. He's been walking for years with that lamb on his back. Of course, it's too abstract or whatever to see any detail on the guy's face. It's like a big stick-figure sculpture. It's more like a sculpture of a skeleton carrying a lamb-skeleton than a real man and a real lamb. They look like the ashy ghosts after some terrible blast. It always looked imminently breakable.

Don't you see, Mom—Peter thinks, continuing a conversation long after the phone's gone dead—I don't even need to go to the reunion because I can see it in my head. I've been reuniting with all of those people in my head for years, and the idea of standing around and trying to report how my life has gone in the past ten years is a task too difficult to endure. I just can't stand to hear all the success stories, honestly. Besides, they never were that interested in me in the first place and any interest they have for me now would be triggered merely by nostalgic good will or by alumni pity and would thereby be fraudulent, and I can do without their pity. I've made it ten years, haven't I?

Don't you see I'm trying to forget these people? Don't you see I'm tired of thinking about it all? All those goddamned people that you grew up with follow you around for so damned long. I'm just hauling them with me wherever I go—Jackson, Memphis, D.C., Florida—I'm tired of carrying all this goddamned weight. Acting all happy on the quad will only make it worse.

೮೫

"What's this?" Tubbel asks, shutting the fridge and holding onto Peter's last good beer. "You got the invite on the fridge."

He pulls the card down.

"I always thought that sculpture was weird," Tubbel says. He tosses the card onto the kitchen counter. "Scary."

"So seriously, listen, you should ride down with me," he says.

"What? You're kidding," Peter says.

"No way. I'm headed straight there. Mary's got family in town so I'm solo. I'm meeting up with Anderson. Everyone'll be there. Jeremy, Anderson, Daniel, all bringing their significants. It's going to be huge. Hiram Stevens says there's even going to be an after thing at Becca Cartright's. Remember her?"

"Yeah."

"That's what I'm saying here: it's going to be the bomb."

"Look that's really nice. But I just don't think I can swing it."

"Seriously. Can't swing it? When's gonna be the next time you can swing it? Really, we'll all be there. No weddings. You're going to be a lawyer soon. We're going to have a baby. Then there won't be time for shit. Come on."

"Seriously, Tubbel. I can't."

He drinks his beer hard, bottle uptilted, his eyes on Peter still.

"So what's your damage lately?" he says.

"Damage?"

"Yeah. Seriously. We haven't seen you since Jeremy's wedding."

"Who's we?"

"Us. We. The guys. Who else? You know, your friends."

"Look, you know how busy everything's been."

"You didn't even come home last Christmas and hell *every*body was home last Christmas. It was fucking great."

"Look. You know I don't have to tell you how hard everything's been."

"Ah, Jesus, Peter, don't pin this on your father, okay? You know we all feel for you, but God," he says, and then *sotto voce*, his lips wet with beer, "it's been what, four years since he died? How long are you going to hold onto this?"

"That's real easy for you to say, Tubbel."

"You know you want to go to this, Pete. You know you'll have fun. I don't get what your deal is about being afraid to see everyone."

"I'm not afraid to see everyone. That's ridiculous. Did my Mom put you up to this?"

He laughed. "No, brainiac. I was driving through town on my way to Jackson. Memphis is in between St. Louis and Jackson, remember?"

"Look, I'm not afraid to see people. I just have things to do here. I have a life here."

"Really? I need a better reason, Pete, honestly."

Just then the toilet flushed, its gush behind the wall sounding like a wall full of pocket change falling out.

"You got somebody back there?" Tubbel asked.

"Yeah. I've got this"—the word sputters in his throat—"friend over."

The girl appears in the hall, a vague figure in the shadows. They're both staring at her and she walks into the lighted kitchen.

"Your friend's still here, huh?" she says to Peter. "Hi, I'm Erin," she says, extending her hand to Tubbel. She's barefoot in loose old jeans and a red T-shirt that's thin and fraying. The shirt is a parody of a Coke logo, with the words *Pike* in that big swirly Coca-Cola font and *Is It* underneath in small, uninflected font. She's still braless, Peter notices. He can tell by the subtle liveliness of her breasts under the shirt, the slight quiver they have and the way he can almost decipher the nipple underneath the shading cloth. Her hair is pulled back and thrown up and stabbed with a pen, a dirty blonde plume, and her jeans are frayed and whitened at the foot, scrunched and soiled from always being underheel.

"Hey, nice to meet you. I'm Jack Tubbel. Ol' Petey didn't tell me you were hiding back there."

"Oh, you know. Just studying," she says.

"What you studying?"

"Oh, just class stuff."

"Over at Sutchfield?"

"Yeah."

"Cool. Good school."

"Peter, if it's okay," she says, "I'm going to start the Branagh back."

"Yeah, that's fine," Peter says. "I'll catch up in a minute."

She walks back into the hall and shuts the door. "Who the hell was that?" Tubbel asks.

"She's just a friend."

"Right. A friend with privileges. *Now* I understand."

"It's not like that, Tubbel."

"Right. Have I met her before? She looks like—"

"Beats me, man. I hardly know her."

"She looks like someone from home. Wait. What's her name?"

"Erin," Peter says. "Her name is Erin."

"Wilson, right?"

"What?"

"That's Erin Wilson. She's a sophomore, right?"

"Yeah, I guess that's her name."

"Holy shit, that's Binc Wilson's little sister."

"Really?"

"Fuck yeah, really."

Peter was silent.

"You're fucking dating Binc Wilson's little sister."

"Whoa, who said anything about dating? We're just friends."

"Right. Right. I can't believe this. Daniel is going to absolutely shit."

"Do you really have to tell Daniel?"

"You must have known who she was, right?"

"How am I supposed to know? It's not like I know *every*thing about *every*body we went to school with, okay?"

"Right. Whatever. I still can't believe you're sleeping with her."

"Tubbel, can you keep it down please?"

"Oh holy shit, man. He was such an asshole."

"I know, Tubbel."

"Of *course* you know. What were you thinking?"

Peter pauses. The bottle is clean except for the foamy dregs. Tubbel's not entirely joking with him.

"I don't know," Peter finally says. "It just kinda happened."

"Where did she come from?"

"I don't know. She goes to school here."

"Yeah, she goes to your old school."

"Yes, I know. She goes to Sutchfield. And she's majoring in theater. You happy now? What did you expect? We're in Midtown for chrissakes. There's nobody else *in* Midtown but theater chicks and queers."

"Yeah and where did she go to high school?"

"Don't play stupid, Tubbel."

"Just say it," he says.

"Why?"

"I just want to hear it," he says.

"She went to Niskayuna, okay?"

"Egg-zactly."

"Exactly what?"

"I don't know. This is just so, so perfect."

"What?"

"You. And her. Dating."

"We're *not* dating."

"Fine. Fine. Fucking, whatever."

"*Hey.*"

"Oh, don't be so high and mighty. Partly I'm just glad you're getting some. Why'd you think I wanted to take you to the reunion so much anyway? But did you really have to go cradle-robbing?"

"*Hey.*"

"Alright, but seriously. Why Erin Fucking Wilson?"

"We're just friends."

Tubbel again makes a face.

"Fine. You're just friends. She sure didn't look like that when we were in school."

"Yeah."

"Who'd a thought ten years ago you'd be watching movies with Binc Wilson's little goddamned sister."

Peter says nothing.

"Oh, Jesus, I'm just joking with you. Mostly." He uptips the bottle and tries to suckle the foam. He knocks it back on the counter. "I gotta piss like crazy."

Peter walks into the hall under the sound of Tubbel pissing. The door to the bedroom is cracked. Funny how the doors in these old Midtown apartments never really close. And how they all have the old glass doorknobs, the ones that turn like cars without power steering.

She's on the papasan, one hand levitating near her head with a cigarette, her hair still floating up spikily above her skull. On screen a blond Kenneth Branagh is sneering at his own reflection. All of Peter's contraband heaped upon the bed reminds him how he should clean his sheets later.

Back to the kitchen he tosses the beer bottle in the recycling and goes to wipe the water rings off the counter. He sees the two pictures, the Good Shepherd and the baby. The Good Shepherd has always looked apocalyptic to him, terribly dismal and postindustrial, and the sonogram just looks like the inside of some dark cloud, all too real (once he deciphers the hand and face again) and all too fake, this blurred abstraction automatically freighted with such significance.

He hears the tumbling quarters of the toilet again and thinks how Tubbel's pride showed through his face—unstoppable. The thought of Tubbel having a child kicks at Peter now that he's alone for a moment. It's like the inside of his chest has just fallen, like some elevator cut from its cords and descending into his gut. He never thought Tubbel would be the first father among them, but then really he never thought any of them would be fathers. For such a long time impregnation was merely the evidence of the most careless mistake.

Maybe this architecture he's been building for adulthood might be wrong, he thinks. Maybe this professional scaffolding he's been fitfully building might not hold enough, if anything. He'd always thought that the job would make him grown up— enough of all this educationally induced adolescence. But what if it took so much more? What if it took a birth to force out the man?

Tubbel walks out. "Well, Mr. Peter. I'd best be hitting it if I want to make the shindig." And then, more quietly, without the stab at being jovial, he says, "So seriously, do you want to come with me?"

"Why?"

"Because it'll be fun. Because I'm your friend, you idiot. We're all your friends. And all of us will be there. All of us assholes you grew up with. Remember us?"

"Tubbel," Peter says, sighing and rubbing his face, "I just—"

"It would be good for you to see us, I think," he says. "How about it? We could be there in three hours flat. We don't even have to tell your mom you're in town. Crash at my Mom's."

"Tubbel," Peter says, "I think you should head on."

"Peter."

"I'm serious, Tubbel. It's not for me."

Tubbel just stands there staring right at him, so Peter looks off at something in the living room. Peter can't tell if Tubbel's angry or resigned or what. He seems for once unreadable.

"All right then. You're the boss," he says. "But I think you might need to get some shit straightened out."

"What shit?"

"I don't know. I can't even really tell. But I've known you long enough to know you're not right, and you need to get looked at. Or something."

"Well, thanks for the perceptive advice."

"Hey, I'm just one friend shooting straight to another friend."

"Well thanks so much, friend."

"All right, all right," he says, back in his jovial buddy voice. He walks to the counter. Peter leans back against the sink.

"Which one of these is mine?"

He picks up both pictures and holds them together for a second and says, "Hmm. Spooky," and hands the postcard of the shepherd to Peter.

"Here's yours. I got mine. Kind of like Garbage Pail Kids, right?"

"Yeah, right," Peter says.

He locks the door behind Tubbel and goes to the window. He can hear Tubbel's steps in their descending intensity down the stairs. It's still raining so the glass is all creamy in the twilight. Parked across the street, Tubbel's truck continuously melts. Tubbel comes into view, his head bent down to the rain, his hair already combed with the wetness but his footsteps unhurried, his shoulders flat and wide under his suitcoat.

Tubbel, who had always been tall, has grown out of his boyhood fatness and now has an appealing ranginess to his arms and legs, his elbows and shoulders and knees somehow more defined. Watching him quickly take off his coat and bow his head and get into his car, Peter thinks really for the first time in his life that he is being surpassed by his friends, that his boys are leaving him, if they'd really ever been with him, that they are all flying away, exploding from the nucleus that is their hometown, spread out like bright cosmic shrapnel across the map while Peter stays close, caught in his tight orbit.

The streetlights come on, bright but then pointillist in the wet window. Tubbel's truck pulls out of the parking lot, its headlights casting rods through the falling rain. Peter worries Tubbel can see him.

Peter thinks of the sonogram, the blurring image of the baby it represents, hidden in Tubbel's wife's belly—still unborn, still unsullied, still unsexed. They used to trade the cards in fourth grade: Blow Hardy, Adam Bomb, Louise Trapeze. Jeremy and

Tubbel always kept theirs pristine, the corners still sharp, the faces unsmudged, just as perfect as the set of Upper Deck baseball cards they each got every Christmas and left unopened, for their protection. Peter's own meager stash he kept in his pocket, but they always became soiled by the pocket trash of the day, dented by his house key or their corners pulled by his worried fingers. Grim Kim, Ampu-Ted, Smellin' Helen. He's amazed he can remember so much about them just from Tubbel's joke, his visit like a light shown into an abandoned cave.

It was college when Tubbel shot up and stretched out. Before, his fatness was as much a part of him as his blond hair and his bad jokes. He was a jiggling water balloon of flesh that was as pale as a girl's neck in winter. He'd been fat as long as anyone could remember. But still, Tubbel never minded going shirtless. He'd shake his pregnant white belly like the kid in *Goonies,* reveling in everyone's hooting, everyone laughing both at him and in awe of him, in the glow of his untrammeled, 13-year-old self, sloshing his stomach for his friends, overstuffed since birth with happiness.

"Peter, honey, lover," the girl calls from the bedroom, "come sit with me."

But he can't hear her. He's not even there. He's in Tubbel's pregnant belly, safe inside the car, borne home once more.

Baggage Claim

Good idea, this new house. Probably bought sometime when Sarah was still in college. A smart move though, everything on the old side of the interstate slowly rotting, like the sun sets a half-hour earlier over there, the winter an extra ten degrees colder, everything. Their old house had bothered me, the way it was set on concrete blocks, small squat pillars every eight feet or so, so that a crack of darkness was always visible underneath, even when it was bright out. It seemed like such an insubstantial way to support a house, like if you leaned on it hard, everything would go all rhombus and bust. But that's how all the houses were over there, back then.

Sunday afternoon. Worst time of the week for a visit like this. Everyone coming off church heading into Sunday football, getting ready for the real church—that church of organized violence. I'd heard that Sarah did get to cheer in college, like she'd always wanted. Always sounded like such a stupid thing to want to do with your life—cheer. Though I can see her doing it, and bet she kept wearing that cross, small, gold, breakable, always just below the clavicle, constant with every outfit. Back in school she'd even worn it with her cheer uniform, and I always thought that odd, that pleated tease of a skirt and that dainty cross. Cheering and Jesus. Cheering *for* Jesus. Praying for cheer.

So much for not thinking today.

My hand's still sore from the accident, still not sure how to explain it. When I get back to Memphis, Erin's sure to ask questions. How to explain how it just seemed right, after coming home from the reunion Friday, feeling all bloaty, and everything about life seeming clear and unfair. The drywall'll patch just fine. I can probably do it before my mother notices. I'll buy mud on the way home, none in the garage. That's the bad thing about widows: they lose their husbands and then they stop stocking everything.

Sarah's mother opens the door, hair bright red, not at all like I remember, and she's got a big smile on, big but tired. Before I know it I've said like half a dozen sentences, small talk all, and I'm sitting on an ottoman with my knees up to my ears, and she's telling me the story about how she and the new husband got this house, how the contract almost fell through, termites in the flooring, everything.

Been a long time. When we were in school her hair was this dirty blonde, a dye job slowly growing out. But now it's a deep rust, kind of aggressive, hair that's not ashamed of being dyed. It's obviously a brand new thing. Probably part of the coping process.

She offers me iced tea, says she remembers me DJing the pep rallies back in high school. Says it was so nice of me to do that back then, though it's not like I didn't charge them for it. Perhaps she doesn't remember that part. The glass of tea is already condensating all over the place, just this slippery tube now in my hand. She thanks me so much for coming, the outpouring of affection from everyone these past three weeks was just amazing, she says.

I've promised myself that in no way will I cry. I've come here for a reason and I'm not going to get all weepy like this glass here and dissolve all over this poor woman.

Of course I never did learn how to DJ for real, just had the gear, bought cheap from a bass player over at Murrah who needed the money for college. There's one guy around town who does it for real, used to do raves for that certain element of public school white kids, the ones with extra earrings who tattooed their notebooks. Music didn't even start until eleven. I went with Tubbel who knew the guy, Tubbel who knew everyone, Tubbel the only friend from Niskayuna High who never changed—in his 20s and still air drumming with no irony. We were home

from school one weekend. We were probably the oldest ones
there. A knot of sweaty arms is all I remember and the music,
consistently throbby, a sexy type of nausea. Somewhere down
Capitol Street at a bar on the second floor, a bar never seen
before, never seen since. We got behind the speakers to hang out
with Dax, the friend. Dax never quit moving, enjoying his own
private dance, internally rocking. He slid the headphones over
his baby ears, then slid them off, hung them around his neck so
that the device looked like some primitive's necklace. We
watched him spin and I drank and Tubbel stuttered happily,
asked him if he had this, if he was going to play that. Dax'd take
the spent disk while the new one played and sleeve it. The floor
was mined with milk crates of LPs, strange plain labels, so many
slices of experience waiting to be called up. He'd pluck a new
one, spear through its cycloptic hole, spin it silently while the
other disc percolated. Dax'd listen, head phones on, face down
close to the disk, light shining off of it in its spinning, light
turning to liquid, turning wheeled into a twisting, a potter's clay.
He'd wait 'til it got up to the right point and blend it over—I had
no idea how he determined this. Each new song seemed just a
mechanical variation on the one before with some added sound
texture, some new noise machine scarring the surface of the beat.
And the people out front writhed completely, afire with some
unseen force. For them, there was no time, no partitions in the
sound, just an endless beating now. Nothing was divided into

tracks of the past. Of course Dax made it seem so, slowly colliding the sound. Like your car's blinker and the car's blinker just in front of you, how yours gradually catches up to theirs and for a moment your light and their light beat as one light until the sync unlocks and you speed ahead.

So much for not thinking today. The problem is that everything always reminds me of everything else.

It's like this one time I was at a four-way stop and for some reason listening to Oldies 94. Diana Ross and the Supremes were singing *Baby, baby baby, where did our love go* and I was singing along—I mean, it's a classic for a reason. I looked up and saw— just for a moment—the mouths of the three other drivers. They were all singing the song. Every throat was wrapped around the *baby baby* at the same time but before the phrase was over someone was revving through the intersection.

Sometimes I think back to that night long ago with Sarah, and I wonder if the music is what made me do it, if it somehow triggered me, and my hands and feet were just amplifying what it told me. But I realize that this is probably not the case.

This glass of iced tea is still crying. Wet, slick, sliding through my hands, I'm holding a solid tube of iced tea. I drink it to make it less heavy. I'll die if I drop this on her floor. It's slowly wetting the uncoastered glass table. Keep the hurt hand to your side, I lecture myself. Don't let it think it can hold the glass. Sarah's mother is talking about how happy she was in college, about how proud she was to cheer, about how she was doing so well until she tore her ACL for the second time, about how that year was made better by The Josh, whom she wouldn't have even met in that Chem Lab if she hadn't stopped cheering and gotten serious about Pre-Pharmacy. No kids yet, she says, eyes brimming, then receding, my glass crying for her. She never cries outright. The tears accumulate and then recede, rushing to her eyelid and then back away like seatide. The Josh is currently staying with his parents, in Memphis. He's not sure what he'll do next. Their pictures are spread all about us—a shoebox exploded. He looks like your average good Southern boy—longish hair on the top, wide-cheeked and wide-shouldered, his frame always gripped nicely tight in his Polo. He has metabolized the calories of college with finesse. He is typically typical. He is me.

He was on a business trip—he works in corporate finance, low level but climbing, already in the routine of full-day cube work and weekends stuffed with TV sports—when it happened. The fire had begun in the basement. They suspected the laundry room, decades of trapped lint. Quickly spread to adjacent storage closet, which served as the landlord's walk-in filing cabinet. Quickly spread to first floor, smoke moving up the elevator shaft. Quickly. Sarah had died from smoke inhalation. The doctors speculated that she had slept through the blaze, hopefully, as she was on a nightly dosage of Ibuprofen and Ambien, as her knees had been bothering her of late, stored joint exhaustion from years of cheering, which had been acting up ever since The Josh had begun traveling frequently, which her mother says was probably psychosomatic, though also awfully sweet. She says all of this almost detached, rehearsed and re-performed enough that it only glosses the trauma, the near-hysterical bodily revolt at the news, the majority of her sadness numbed by three weeks of the shock and awe of it, of the demeaning goodwill of guests, the constant telling and retelling, knitting and reknitting so many religious sayings in the face of this end time.

We Niskayuna grads have already set up a college scholarship in her name for some plucky cheerleader. Her mother is so proud, goes on and on about the $22,000 we've already raised. I'd had no idea it was so much. All I remember about Friday is drinking beer and stuffing money into a goddamned hat.

"All of you Niskayuna grads have done so well, professionally. And in other ways," she says.

Oh and we were such a hearty bunch, married and procreating like hell, steadily fattening into our parents' shadows. She's heard from so many good people these last few weeks, so many wonderful things to remember, she says, resting her eyes on me, and I wonder if she's understood why I'm here. But her face feels somehow hollow or if not hollow, then not completely there, as if she's just the papered husk of herself and the real warm cells of herself are hiding behind the walls of the house, grieving like insulation.

"I wanted to come and see you," I say. "To pay my respects. To apologize."

"Well, I so appreciate you coming, Peter, but what do you have to apologize for? You were always so sweet to everyone. I'm sorry you didn't get to meet her Josh. I think you two would've been great friends."

"He sounds like a nice man, like he treated her well."

"He did—so much so," she says, almost breaking down here, and I set the glass down, one hand wet with dew and the other swollen thick and throbbing.

"But you don't have to apologize. You've paid me a visit. I don't see how you have anything to worry about. None of us have anything to worry about. Everyone has been so kind ..."

"But no, I do need to apologize, Mrs. Samson." And immediately I feel the tinge of bad manners, calling her by her old name. "I do. I—my relationship with your daughter, with her, with Sarah, it wasn't always perfect. I did things. I said things. Things that I'm not proud of."

"Oh honey, you're such a sweetheart. It's all water under the bridge. I know where you're coming from. Even her Josh has confessed to me, of thoughts he'd had, worries—they were so close to having children—everyone's got this urge, to voice every dark thought they might have had, but I promise it's okay. All's forgiven now, so sayeth Our Savior. I really wouldn't worry. Just saying that you had a cross word aloud, just mentioning it to me makes it vanish. It makes it all better. You should feel better. She feels better now."

Pictures of Sarah and The Josh cover the coffee table: Sarah and Josh drinking ornate margaritas in Mexico, Sarah and Josh all scarfed up outside some football stadium, Sarah and Josh cutting a rug at their wedding, her shoes kicked off somewhere out of the frame, her fists pulling up the hem of her dress and all that complex cobwebby lace underneath. I rigorously guard the pictures from my sweaty glass of tea and its pathetic puddle.

"She's in a better place," her mother says, "and though it hurts me to even talk about it, I know she is up there, watching, and she hears us right now, and she waiteth for me."

She speaks slow and sure, her glassy brown eyes tearless now and certain. Her hands cradle her own iced tea. She doesn't reach out to touch me, to lay upon the hands, no Bible conspicuously out, but I can tell she means it, that she's steeled by something invisibly strong, just like Sarah all those years ago.

"No, I know," I say. "But I mean, what I did, back in high school, back at that dance. I never said. I've never said to anyone..."

She stares straight, her gaze now changed. She's gone perplexed, inquisitive. For the first time since I've been there. She has no idea what I'm talking about.

"There was a dance," I say. "Our senior year."

"I'm sorry, hon. I don't remember. What dance was this?"

"It was prom," I say. "It was our senior prom."

It comes sudden, an impacting pain, like when I hit the wall Friday night after the reunion, a momentary painless present void and then the sharp and swelling fact of it, the cracked knuckle, the inner invisible shattering up my arm—Sarah never told her. She has no idea what happened back then.

"It was—you're right—it was nothing," I say.

"No, tell me," she says. "I want to know. I want to know everything, everything anyone has ever said to her or heard her say or anything. It's all I've got now. Please, tell me. It will make everyone feel better."

She has no idea. It helps explain why I never got in trouble, at least in any adult way. All of the students steered completely clear of me for the rest of the year after it happened, just knew I was an unhinged psychopath ready to go postal at any moment, pull a Columbine or something. I started to eat my lunch in my car every day, so amazingly isolated, just me and a sandwich and the car radio. But in all that talk and squabble, Sarah, whom I'd never spoken to again afterward, didn't tell anyone, kept it in. I wonder if, in those exploratory months of first love, she ever told The Josh about it, ever told him about the guy who was so in love with her he once followed her into the bathroom, at prom, and attacked her.

Was it love? Just who was I in love with back then? Everyone and no one? Why would a boy attack anybody except for true love? Was it instead a type of hatred? I can't tell. The emotion comes so sudden, so overwhelming. It's like my anger problem, as Erin calls it. This feeling—is there a better word than *feeling*?—this feeling jumps down on me from above. Erin says I've got Anger Management Issues. And then so I say, if I've got Management issues, can I take it up with Human Resources? But she never laughs. She's very serious. At some point I stopped being funny to people. She says my anger frightens her. And I think: well, then quit making me angry. But it's like last night with the wall—I don't know why. Thinking isn't part of it. I don't even know how to describe it. That's what Erin's always asking for—for me to talk it out. But I don't want to talk! That's why I punch walls, because it makes more sense than talking. Talking only makes things worse.

Where does this come from? she'll shriek sometimes when it's gotten bad. It just uprushes all sudden, like a flame on a gas stove. It's like a pilot light—always there. If you turn the lights off and crouch down you can see it. It's always a flick of the wrist away from a full flame.

After is always the worst. All the talking, the postgame, the discussion. And I can't quit thinking, ever since Tubbel told me Friday night, when he pulled me aside after I'd gotten there. He was so surprised to see me, and I was ecstatic that I'd done it, changed my mind and made a liar out of myself and shown up, and he looked so sad, as he drug me outside and bummed someone's pack of cigarettes so he could tell me in relative peace what they'd all learned earlier that evening. It's like as soon as he told me all the ideas I've ever had have been screaming inside my head. It's this horrible mindfulness that's killing me. I just want to empty my head—no more words, no more ideas, no more thinking—and that's why hitting walls makes sense. It empties out everything. Everything becomes clear and empty and verbless and light passes through. But then right after, everything rushes back in to fill the hole and I don't know if I'll ever get rid of this new fullness.

"No, it's nothing," I say. "It's just—once there was this dance. And she was there. I hadn't gone to the dance with her. She was with someone else, and I went up to her. I mean, she came up to me and I was ... I was mean to her."

"Mean how?" She looks genuinely curious. Who can blame her?

It's like Sarah's face that night, when she turned around after I came into the bathroom—I can never forget this—the terrible anticipation in her face, wondering what I was about to do.

"I well, see. I had a crush on her. And I don't remember who she was with. I mean going out with. At that time. And anyway—I don't even remember who I was at the dance with— she just asked me to dance, Sarah did, and I guess I was trying to play it cool or something, or hard to get, and well, I just said no, and I told her I didn't want to dance right then, and I think I hurt her feelings, or I know I did. And I've just felt bad, you know, ever since, because I really did want to dance with her. And I don't know why I said I didn't. I don't know why I did so many things, and I just, I've always felt bad about it, I guess, and— God, is this making any sense?"

"Perfect sense, darling," and she's smiling, beaming now, and standing. "Come here," she says, opening her arms. Suddenly she's offering to hug me and like good soldiers my knees get up and stand, and I put the wet tea down and I'm hugging her—so odd to hug a stranger, so intimate, almost more intimate than kissing, all of you upon a whole other person. She hugs me, long, slow, a religious hug. She's happy with my story. It has fulfilled something. She keeps talking low and sweet like you'd talk to a pet.

"It's okay, Peter. It's all going to be okay. She knows you're sorry. She's heard you. She knows you want to dance with her and she still wants to dance with you, too. She's dancing right now, she's dancing with you up above us. She's watching and she's listening and she knows what you're thinking and what you've said and it's all going to be all right. She's dancing with you right now and she's waiting. She waiteth on us to join her, which we all will, someday."

And her mother starts to sway, ever so gently, slightly, a shifting of the weight from one bent knee to the other, like her legs are inhaling exhaling, inhaling exhaling, and without even thinking about it I'm crying, the tears just out now and coming down my cheeks, the glass is breaking and her rose-smelling face is humming into me, gently wafting on a wave of *it will be okay it will all be all right my darling dear* cooing into my ear as I weep gently over her shoulder. I can't stop though I so much want to stop, my eyes balled up like fists fighting back, my hands, one wet from the glass and one gnarled and numb and swollen, delicately touching her back, trying to hold myself upright against this sound, her mother—Sarah's mother—this speaker that is her mother.

About the Author

Barrett Hathcock was born and raised in Jackson, Mississippi. He has published fiction and nonfiction in the *Colorado Review*, the *Arkansas Review*, the *MacGuffin*, *Fried Chicken and Coffee*, the *Cimarron Review*, and *REAL: Regarding Arts & Letters*. For the past five years, he has served as a contributing editor for *The Quarterly Conversation*. He received an MFA from the University of Alabama in 2004 and he has taught writing at Samford University and Rhodes College. He lives with his wife and growing family in a house down by the river in Memphis, Tennessee, which is thankfully no longer at flood level.

CPSIA information can be obtained at www.ICGtesting.com
Printed in the USA
LVOW091339181211

259977LV00003B/220/P

9 780982 673485